There was no future for Courtney with him, and she was the kind of woman who deserved a future.

She was young and beautiful and caring and came from a strong, close family.

He was past young, scarred up on the inside, as well as the out, and the only family he knew—or who mattered to him—was the family of Hollins-Winword security agency.

It was a fact of life that was easy enough to remember when he was usually a continent or two away from her.

But sprawled across a bed under her *roof?*

That was an entirely different matter.

She reappeared in the doorway with a gigantic Saint Bernard at her side.

"You didn't get a dog." Mason eyed the shaggy beast. "You got a damn horse."

She grinned, bringing a surprising impishness to her oval face and tucked her long, golden hair behind her ear.

He couldn't take his eyes off her.

Dear Reader,

This year marks the thirteenth year I've been blessed to be able to share the Double-C Ranch "family" with all of you. When I started out, I had no idea what a wonderful adventure it would all turn out to be—and continues to be, every single day. Though I certainly hoped that you would welcome the family into your lives, I could never have come close to understanding how wonderful it would be knowing just what a special home these people would find with you.

Now, here we are again, with Courtney Clay, who is settling into the home and the future she wants to make. And with Mason Hyde—who has as little idea when he starts out how much he wants that home to be with him as I did when I started out more than a decade ago.

And so their adventure begins....

Thank you for being there to share it!

Allison

COURTNEY'S
BABY PLAN

ALLISON LEIGH

Harlequin®

SPECIAL EDITION

Recycling programs
for this product may
not exist in your area.

ISBN-13: 978-0-373-65614-1

COURTNEY'S BABY PLAN

Copyright © 2011 by Allison Lee Johnson

This edition published by arrangement with Harlequin Books S.A.

For questions and comments about the quality of this book please contact us at Customer_eCare@Harlequin.ca.

® and TM are trademarks of Harlequin Books S.A., used under license. Trademarks indicated with ® are registered in the United States Patent and Trademark Office, the Canadian Trade Marks Office and in other countries.

www.Harlequin.com

Printed in U.S.A.

Books by Allison Leigh

ALLISON LEIGH

There is a saying that you can never be too rich or too thin. Allison doesn't believe that, but she does believe that you can *never* have enough books! When her stories find a way into the hearts—and bookshelves—of others, Allison says she feels she's done something right. Making her home in Arizona with her husband, she enjoys hearing from her readers at Allison@allisonleigh.com or P.O. Box 40772, Mesa, AZ 85274-0772.

For my family.

Prologue

It all started with a kiss.

A twenty-dollar kiss, to be precise.

Courtney Clay inhaled carefully and stared up at the man standing outside her apartment door. She didn't *do* this sort of thing...inviting strange men into her home during the wee hours. Or any hour, for that matter.

But then Mason Hyde wasn't entirely a stranger. He was a friend of her cousin's, after all.

And he could kiss like nobody she'd ever met.

The statement whispered through her mind, tempting.

She straightened her fingers, then curled them once more around the doorknob. "Do you want to come in?"

His eyes were deep shadows despite the porch light burning brightly above her front door. "Yes." His voice was deep. Blunt. And—as it had struck her from the first moment she'd encountered him—entrancingly melodious. That first time, when she'd heard him speaking to someone else, she'd thought how his voice didn't seem to quite match his almost dangerous-looking appearance.

The second time, just that afternoon when he'd stopped in front of her kissing booth at the town's Valentine's Day festival, plunked down a twenty for a five-dollar kiss and told her with a crooked smile that she could keep the change, she'd realized just how perfectly his voice *did* fit him.

And even though there had been a narrow table between them on which that twenty-dollar bill rested, she'd felt something curl inside her when he'd spoken. And something curl even more tightly when his eyes had stared into hers.

Her knees had felt a little shaky. Her stomach had danced a little nervously. And her voice had risen about half an octave when she'd thanked him for his generous donation on behalf of the local school that was benefiting from the funds being raised that day.

But then his lips had tilted a little crookedly, which seemed to make the thin scar that slashed down his face from his right temple to his jaw even more apparent, and he'd leaned across the table toward her and brushed his lips gently…simply…across hers.

And that's where her memory stopped dead in its tracks.

The contact of his lips on hers had simply caused every cell in her brain to short-circuit.

Which is what had led them here.

To this moment.

With him standing at her door in the wee hours of the night, exactly twenty minutes after she'd gotten off her shift at the hospital. Exactly where—and when—she'd uncharacteristically invited him, in a rushed, quiet voice, lest anyone else around the kissing booth hear her, after he'd murmured that he'd really like to see her again. Somewhere. Anywhere that didn't involve a line of ten guys—young and old—who were happy to hand over a few bucks to kiss a pretty nurse.

Now, though, despite saying that he did want to come inside, he hadn't moved so much as an inch. Instead, he was watching her intently with those eyes that she knew from the kissing booth were a startlingly pale green against his olive-toned skin.

"Are you sure you want me to come in? I'm not going to want to leave anytime soon. We could go out somewhere. Have some coffee."

She hadn't expected that. Her moist hand tightened around the door handle as she continued looking up at him. She was tall. But he was a whole lot taller. A whole lot broader.

Go somewhere for coffee? Somewhere safe. Somewhere innocuous. Or invite him in?

She didn't have indiscriminate encounters with near strangers. She didn't do anything in her life that wasn't well thought-out. Well planned.

But she didn't want to go to the all-night coffee shop and sit across a table from him pretending that all she wanted was conversation and coffee.

She wanted his long arms wrapped around her.

Wanted to be held against his wide, wide chest.

Wanted his warm lips on hers.

She *wanted*. Period.

More than ever before in her life.

And even though her heart bumped nervously inside her chest, she moved her bare feet, stepping back as she pulled the door fully open.

"Yes." Her voice was soft but clear. "I'm sure."

His lips slowly tilted and he stepped inside.

Without a word, he reached for her with one hand, and with the other, he pushed the door closed.

Chapter One

"No," Mason Hyde said adamantly as he stared up at his boss. And he hoped to hell he showed none of the alarm he was feeling. "You can't fire me."

"You insist on checking yourself out against medical advice and I'll have no choice." Coleman Black's voice was flat. Unmoved. "I don't need stupid agents. What I *do* need is you recovered and healthy, Mase." The gray-haired man frowned and moved across the hospital room, finally showing some emotion—even if Mason figured it was only irritation. "You just had surgery yesterday," Cole pointed out. "And two days before that, you were still in the hospital in Barcelona."

Mason grimaced and looked away. Maybe *stupid* was the perfect word to describe his desperation to get out of the hospital, but if anyone should understand why he needed to get out...get away...it should have been Cole.

Yeah, he was Mason's boss. But he was also Mason's

friend. And Mason didn't have many people in his life that he considered a friend. He had even fewer people in his life who knew his history like Cole did.

"I don't want to end up like I did before," he muttered, and hated that the admission made him feel weak.

Cole glanced at the open door to Mason's room and shook his head. "Maybe if you told the hospital what your history is, *why* you keep refusing the—"

"No." Mason cut the other man off. It had been ten years, for God's sake. But right now, lying there in a hospital bed while pain racked every corner of his body, it felt as if it were just yesterday.

Yesterday, when he'd been in another hospital—only that trip had been courtesy of an explosion rather than a deadly aimed SUV. Then, he'd been shot full of endless painkillers. Painkillers that had become the only thing he'd been able to think about and just about the only thing he'd been able to care about. He'd ended up losing everything—except his job—that really *had* mattered to him.

He'd be damned if he'd head down that road again.

And he'd be damned if he'd admit to anyone now what a hole he'd had to climb out of before. Particularly his doctors. "It has nothing to do with anything now," he muttered.

Cole raised his eyebrows and pointedly eyed the contraption that held Mason's casted left leg at a strange angle above the bed. A triangular bar was also suspended above Mason's chest, allowing the big man something to grab on to with his left hand, since his right was also in a long cast. "I believe the entire medical community would disagree," he said drily. Then he sighed, knowing that there were some arguments that never would work with Mason. The man marched to his own drummer.

The phone inside his lapel pocket was vibrating. Had been ever since he'd walked into Mason's hospital room ten minutes earlier. As the head of Hollins-Winword, he had at least fifty things that needed his immediate attention. Yet he was here, standing in a hospital room having a battle of wills with one of his most talented—and most stubborn—agents.

He stifled a sigh again. It was no coincidence, he supposed, that *talent* and *stubborn* seemed to generally go hand in hand. An agent had to have a strong will to work in the field. Cole didn't want to have anyone under his watch who *didn't* have a strong will.

But right now, that particular trait was causing him no small amount of consternation.

"Well, the doctors are up to you as long as you're inside these walls. But once you go AWOL from this place, your recuperation is up to *me.* And I'm telling you that you don't have a choice. Either you give up the notion of not needing any more medical care, or you won't *have* a job to come back to.

At the best of times, Mason's face was stoic. Cole had known the man since long before he'd acquired the thin scar that extended nearly the entire side of his face, so he knew that basic expression wasn't owed to the scar. And now, given the situation, Mason's face had all of the animation of the grim reaper.

"You can't fire me." Mason's voice was low. Gruff.

Which meant he was actually worried that Cole *would.*

And much as it pained him, that's what they both needed right now. "I can and I will," he assured flatly. Though he wasn't quite sure how. But Cole hadn't gotten to where he was without mastering the art of a bluff. Not that he was bluffing, exactly. He truly did not want to lose Mason as an agent. Whether he was profiling maniacal nuts or invisibly protecting people who weren't easy to protect, the guy had a talent that went miles beyond training. It was instinctive. As if he'd been bred into it.

But more importantly, Cole didn't want to lose Mason, period. And the damn fool was likely to kill himself at the rate he was going.

The annoyance of his buzzing cell finally drove him to pull it out of his pocket and glance at the display. More crises that, at least, had nothing to do with his business with Mason. He pocketed the phone. "Be glad you have alternatives," he continued. "I know Axel Clay has talked to you. Considering everything, getting out of Connecticut and lying low in Wyoming for a few months while you recover seems an excellent idea to me."

Mason slid him a look. Trust Cole to hedge around until he got to the crux of the matter. The older man had obviously been a spy for too damn long. How else had he known that he and Ax had spoken?

He started to reach for the bar to shift in the bed, but just thinking about lifting his arm above his shoulder sent a shock wave down his spine. Instead, he curled his good hand into a fist and breathed through the pain, reminding himself that feeling that pain was a helluva lot better than ending up addicted to painkillers again, and feeling only the uncontrollable urge for *another* numbing pill. "Bugging the hospital telephone, Cole?"

His boss didn't answer that. "His solution is pretty damn perfect, far as I'm concerned. Not only will you be under the watchful eye of a nurse without having to stay in the hospitals you detest, but you'll get some peace from the media hounds here."

"I've had enough of nurses, thanks." At any other time, Mason might—might—have found the double entendre humorous, but right then, he couldn't muster it. "I'll be bored crazy in Wyoming," he lied. Nothing had been boring the last time he'd been there over a year and a half ago.

The other man just shrugged. "Then you get yourself transferred to a twenty-four-hour care center whether you like it or not or you stay here, 'cause you're not going to your own place. I know you. You go to that box you call a home, and you'll do too much before you should and end up back here again even worse off than you are now."

If it weren't for the heavy-duty antibiotics that were being intravenously pumped into him, Mason wouldn't even have to be *in* the hospital. The collision between his body and the SUV he'd jumped in front of had happened a week ago. The most recent surgery that he'd had to finish putting Humpty Dumpty back together again was the last one he was supposed to need. And if he hadn't gotten the infection that necessitated that surgery, his doctors and his nurses would have been glad to see the last of him the minute they'd finished wrapping half his body in plaster.

"Damned if I do, damned if I don't," he muttered. The longer he stayed in the hospital, the worse he felt. But if he left on his own, Cole would cut him off from the only thing that mattered to him.

"I'll check on you tomorrow morning." Obviously unmoved, Cole headed toward the doorway of Mason's private room. "Either have a plan in place or give me your resignation." His voice was hard, and without another glance his way, the man walked out of the room.

Mason leaned his head back and let out a long, colorful oath.

Agents who pushed Cole hard got pushed back hard. And more than a few good ones had ended up walking away from the agency that had been the center of Mason's life for so many years.

He wasn't going to be one of them.

He grimaced and threw his good arm over his eyes. He could feel panic nibbling at the edges of his sanity.

And Mason wasn't a man who panicked.

Admitting it, even to himself, was damn hard.

But not as hard as it had been to kick an addiction that had ruled his life for eighteen months. And right now, ten years or not, he was craving a narcotic numbness as badly as he ever had.

"Good afternoon, Mr. Hyde. How are we feeling today?" The young nurse who came into the room on her squeaking, rubber-soled shoes greeted him in a revoltingly cheerful voice. One corner of Mason's brain had to give the kid credit for maintaining that unswerving cheer when dealing with him.

He *knew* he wasn't an easy patient.

"When you have a dozen broken bones, *we* will talk about it," he said wearily. He wasn't interested in watching her as she fussed around him—even if she was about as cute as a fresh-faced cheerleader—and closed his eyes.

She didn't reply, but he could still hear her moving around and feel her faint touch as she checked this and adjusted that. Which meant maybe the kid did have the ability to learn.

"You know, Mr. Hyde," she said after a moment,

proving that he'd overestimated, "I couldn't help but hear a little bit of your conversation with your visitor."

He opened his eyes and watched her.

She smiled tentatively, looking more than a little nervous. "I was out in the hall waiting to come in and change your IV bag. Anyway," she rushed on, "I'm supposed to help convince you that it's in your best interests to stay with us for a while longer, but I do know some really good nurses who provide home health care if you'd like some names."

He shrugged and held back a curse at the pain the movement caused. "Yeah. Sure." His voice was short. And even though he had no real intention of following up on her well-intentioned list, at least it took the nervousness out of her eyes. She could get on her way and leave him in peace.

She deftly slid the call button into the fingers that protruded below the edge of his cast. "I'll get the names for you. Be sure to call if you change your mind and want something stronger than the OTC stuff for that pain."

He'd chew off his tongue before he asked for anything stronger. He managed a relatively civil grunt in return, and her shoes carried her, squeaking, back out of the hospital room.

When he'd called Cole, he'd hoped to enlist the guy's aid to get out of the hospital. His place wasn't much, but at least he didn't have an ongoing stream of medical professionals bugging him every hour on the hour, and he wouldn't be a call button away from begging for a damn narcotic. His job kept him on the road about fifty weeks out of the year, and his apartment was more a repository for the mail that was shoved through the mail slot than it was a home.

Hell. He didn't even have dishes in his kitchen cupboards. He barely had soap and a towel in his bathroom.

The only thing he'd end up finding at his apartment was more discomfort and a barrage of phone calls from eager reporters who'd regrettably discovered he was the so-called hero who'd saved the life of an internationally known businessman's daughter.

Mason wasn't the only one who was media shy. He didn't want strangers looking into his life, poking and speculating. But he also worked for an agency that preferred operating under the radar. Their primary concern was security—personal and international—and it was beneficial for everyone concerned that their activities not be looked at too closely by an inquisitive public. Particularly since HW generally operated with the government's tacit approval. They handled the stuff that the elected boys and girls couldn't—or didn't want to—get caught up in.

Unfortunately, Donovan McDougal—or someone from his sizable camp—had opened their mouth to the wrong person about Mason's involvement in McDougal's personal security, and even though Cole had done his best to get a lid on it, the newshounds were busy sniffing out the story behind the near-tragic "accident."

He let the call button fall out of his grip and reached out for the hospital phone that was on a rolling stand beside the bed. His cell phone had been decimated by the vehicle that had hit him. He'd had no opportunity to replace it yet, but he had a good memory for numbers. He dragged the corded, heavy phone closer with his good arm so he could punch out the numbers.

Axel answered on the second ring.

"Set it up," was all Mason said. Then he let the receiver clatter back in place.

Going along with Axel's idea might keep Mason in Cole's good graces, but that didn't mean it was a good idea. Yeah, Ax's cousin was a registered nurse. Yeah, she'd recently bought a house and wanted to pick up some extra money.

From the outside, it might seem like a win-win situation. Courtney Clay padded her bank account, and Mason got Cole off his back.

But none of them knew about the night that Mason had spent in Courtney's bed over a year and a half ago. A memorable night. The kind of night that haunts a man.

But it had only been one night. He'd known that going in, he'd known it when he'd walked away the morning after and also when, during the days that followed, he'd had to fight the urge to contact her again.

Women like Courtney Clay were better off without guys like Mason Hyde in their lives.

Even she had agreed to that particular fact.

He was surprised that she'd gone along with her cousin's suggestion to not only give Mason room and board now but to also provide him with whatever nursing care he needed until he could take care of himself.

But maybe she hadn't been as haunted as he'd been by that night together. Maybe it made no difference to her one way or another who her temporary roommate was going to be. Maybe it was just about the money.

It didn't seem to fit what he knew about her. But then, what he knew most about her was what her lips tasted like. What her smooth, honey-tinted skin felt like beneath his fingertips.

She'd been the one to invite him to her place that long-ago day. He'd been in Weaver for a few days helping Axel out on a case. And though Mason had made it plain he wanted to see her again, he'd had no expectation, no plan, that it would lead to her bed.

She was too young for him, but she was an incredibly beautiful woman. Turning down that particular opportunity had even occurred to him. Until she'd whispered for him not to worry. It was just one night. She'd said those words herself.

So when she'd stared up at him in the shadowy light of her living room and began unbuttoning her blouse, he'd helped her finish the job.

He'd made the mistake of forgetting who and what he was when he'd tried to have a normal life eleven years ago. He wasn't going to do it again.

Not even when the temptation came in the form of a shapely, blonde nurse whose touch still hung in his memory.

He was in a wheelchair.

Even though Courtney had expected it, the sight of Mason sitting in the chair made her wince inside.

"Remember what you're doing this for," she whispered to herself. She needed to keep her long-term plan in the forefront of her mind. It would be the only way she could get through the short-term…awkwardness.

She gave a mental nod and drew in a quick, hard breath as she brushed her hands down the front of her pale pink scrubs. Then she pulled the door wide and stepped out onto her porch to watch her cousin push Mason's wheelchair up the long ramp that her brother had finished building just that morning over the front and back steps so that once her boarder did arrive, they'd be more easily able to get him in and out of the house.

She realized she couldn't quite look Mason in the

face and focused instead on her cousin. "Everything go okay with the flight out from Connecticut?"

"How would he know?" Mason answered before Axel could. His pale green gaze drew hers. "He wasn't the one cooped up on the plane."

A frown pulled his slashing eyebrows together over his aquiline nose. Combined with the dark shadow of beard on his jaw—evidence that he hadn't shaved in at least a few days—he looked thoroughly put out.

She lifted an eyebrow and managed a calm smile. "Feeling a little cranky, are we?"

"What is it with you nurses and the eternal *we*?"

"Ignore him," Axel advised as he pushed the wheelchair past her into the house. He pulled a fat, oversized envelope from beneath his arm and handed it to her. "He's been bitching since I picked him up in Cheyenne. Here're his meds."

Courtney took the envelope and looked inside at the various prescription bottles it contained. She'd already reviewed a copy of her new patient's medical chart. It had been faxed to her yesterday after Axel had called her out of the blue to ask if she was interested in taking on a home health care patient.

She'd done similar work before. Just not when the patient in question was living under her roof. But the money he'd said the patient would pay had been enough to get her interest, and in a hurry.

It was only after she'd agreed and had asked how he knew the patient that she'd learned *who* her new roomie was going to be.

There was no earthly way, at that point, that Courtney would have been able to back out without explaining to her cousin why. And she had no intention of sharing those particular details.

So, she'd squelched her reservations and reviewed the file when it arrived. Even though she was trained for objectivity, she'd been horrified at the injuries that Mason had sustained. She also hadn't been able to help wondering how on earth he'd been hurt, but that particular information had not been in his chart.

Which meant it was probably work related.

She was ridiculously familiar with the hush-hush aura surrounding the company that Mason worked for, because it was the same company that many of her relatives had worked for. Or still did.

Of course she wasn't supposed to know much about Hollins-Winword. But she wasn't an idiot. She had ears that worked perfectly well. The first time she'd heard the name, she'd been a schoolgirl. As she'd gotten older, she'd discerned more.

And then when Ryan went missing…

She broke off the thought. It was pointless reliving the misery of believing her big brother was dead, because he was home now. Safe and sound, miraculously enough a newlywed with a family of his own.

She followed Axel and Mason into the house and nudged the door closed behind her as she studied the labels on the prescription bottles. Various industrial-strength antibiotics and vitamins and minerals. When she got to the last bottle, though, she frowned a little.

She'd read in Mason's file that he refused to take prescription-strength pain medication, yet that's exactly what she was looking at.

There was nothing in his file about drug allergies, so—if he was anything like the men in her family—it was probably more likely some macho belief that real men didn't need anything to take the edge off their pain, even if it was only for a few days.

She dropped the narcotic back in the envelope and stepped around Mason's protruding leg cast. She set the envelope on the square dining room table near the arch separating the great room from the kitchen and turned toward the men. "Your room is at the end of the hall." Meeting Mason's gaze only made her skin want to flush, so she focused on the few stray, silver strands glimmering among the dark brown hair that sprang back thick and straight from his forehead. "The bathroom is next to it. You *are* able to manage with crutches, aren't you?"

"It's not pretty, but yeah." He sounded marginally less cranky than before, and Courtney couldn't help but feel a rush of sympathy for the man.

No matter what had transpired between them that Valentine's night, the man was recovering from several serious injuries. He had matching long, blue casts on his right arm and his left leg. She also knew that he'd suffered several bruised ribs. He was in pain and, for now, was having to depend on someone else to help him with basic functions from bathing to eating. Of course he was cranky.

Anyone would be.

She looked at her cousin. "Why don't you bring in the rest of his things, and I'll get Mason settled in bed." She could feel heat climbing her neck at that. She didn't bother waiting for Axel to respond but moved next to him and nudged his hands away from the wheelchair so she could push it herself.

Last night, before she'd gone on duty at the hospital, she'd rearranged some of the furniture in her living area to accommodate Mason. Her experience with him told her that he wasn't the least bit clumsy. But Mason was a big man and, clumsy or not, he had a cast covering one leg from foot to thigh. That, combined with the cast on his opposing arm, meant he'd need all the space he could maneuver in, whether by wheelchair or by crutches.

The wheels on the chair squeaked slightly against the reclaimed-wood, planked floor as she pushed him down the hall, hesitating only briefly when they passed the bathroom. "Tub with a shower," she told him in the most neutral nurse's voice she could muster.

"Don't tease me. Only thing I get these days is a wet washcloth."

She felt heat in her throat again as she turned his chair slightly and carefully pushed him into the spare bedroom. "Sorry. I imagine a real shower is something you're looking forward to."

He made a grunting sound in reply.

After angling the chair alongside the bed, she moved around it. She'd already pulled the covers back, and the pillows were stacked up against the wrought-iron head-board. There was also an old recliner from her parents that Ryan had muscled into one corner of the room.

She stopped in front of Mason. He was wearing a white T-shirt that strained at his shoulders and a pair of gray sweatpants with one leg split up the side to accommodate the cast. His toes below the cast were bare, and he had on a scuffed tennis shoe on his other foot.

And he still managed to make her mouth water. Which was not what a nurse should be thinking about her patient, she reminded herself. "Ready to get out of the chair?"

He looked no more enthusiastic than she felt. "You're not strong enough to lift me."

"Not if you were dead weight," she allowed. "But you're not. So which do you prefer? Bed or chair?"

He didn't look at her. "Bed."

Which he probably took as some admission of weakness. Coming from a family of strong individuals, that, too, was something with which she had plenty of familiarity. "All right." Before she could let her misgivings get in the way, she locked the wheels and removed the arm of the wheelchair. Then she bent her knees close to his and grasped him loosely around the waist, leaving room for him to brace his good leg beneath him as she lifted. "Ready?"

He gave another grunt, putting out his uninjured hand against the mattress, so he could add his own leverage. "Just do it."

She tightened her arms, lifting with her legs, and held back her own grunt as she took his weight for the brief moment before he got his leg beneath him. Then he was out of the chair, pivoting more or less smoothly until he landed on the bed, sitting.

She held on to him only long enough to be certain that he wasn't going to tip over, before she straightened. Her stomach was quivering nervously, but the sight of his pale face and tight lips took precedence. "I know," she murmured. "Not very pleasant. But it'll get better."

His expression shifted from pain to *pained.* "I don't need coddling."

She gave him the kind of stern look she'd learned from her grandmother. Gloria was retired now, but she'd been a nurse, and it was in that capacity that she'd met Courtney's grandfather, Squire Clay. And she'd had plenty of years since then to refine that stern look and pass it on to her granddaughters. "Believe me," she assured him, "you won't *get* coddling from me. Now, do you want to sit there on the side of the bed or lean back?" She didn't wait for an answer before she reached down for his casted leg.

But his hands brushed against hers as he did the same, and she had to suck down another shock of tingles that ripped through her. She moved her hand from beneath his. Feeling shaky again, she deftly tucked a wedge of foam, which she'd gotten from the hospital, beneath his leg and stepped away, while he swore and jabbed at the pillows propped behind him.

Sweat had broken out on his brow.

She curled her fingers, fighting the urge to help him as he awkwardly shifted, lest he mistake her assistance for the banned coddling. "What can I get you to make you more comfortable?"

He finally settled, his head leaning against the headboard behind him. He shoved his hand through his hair and looked up at her. "I don't suppose sex is one of the options, is it?"

Chapter Two

Courtney stared, and the heat that she'd been trying to keep at bay flooded hot and furious into her cheeks. "Excuse me?"

"You want me to repeat it?"

Her lips parted. She wanted to say something, but there just weren't any words that were coming to mind.

And then there wasn't time, because Axel came into the room and dumped a very worn leather duffel bag on the floor next to the foot of the bed. He also had a pair of metal crutches that he propped against the wall near the doorway. "I'd hang around and shoot the breeze," he told them both, "but Tara's got an appointment this afternoon and I'm on Aidan-duty. Hard to believe how much one fourteen-month-old kid can get around." He pulled a slender cell phone out of his back pocket and handed it to Mason. "Courtesy of Cole," he told him, before bumping knuckles with Mason's fist and hustling out of the room.

A second later, they heard the front door open and close.

Courtney held her tongue between her teeth and looked back at Mason. "No," she finally said, breaking the thick silence. "Sex is not an option. Obviously."

His gaze trapped hers, but she couldn't tell if he was amused or not. "Because you think I'm presently incapable, or because I didn't call you the morning after?"

She shoved her curling fists into the pockets of her scrubs. She didn't even want to entertain ideas of what Mason was capable or incapable of doing. "I didn't ask you to call me," she reminded. Not the morning after, nor during the twenty months that had passed since then. "You're here because you're recovering from an assortment of injuries. Period."

The corner of his lips lifted a fraction. "Yeah, that's what I expected but figured we might as well get it out of the way so you can stop looking worried that I'm going to bring it up."

Ordinarily, she preferred being straightforward, too. But right now, she wished she could keep up the pretense that nothing had ever occurred between them. "Number one—" she leaned over and picked up his duffel bag "—I wasn't worried. And number two, now it's out of the way. Subject done." She hefted the surprisingly heavy bag onto the empty surface of the dresser and glanced at him over her shoulder. "I'll unpack this if you don't mind?"

His lips twisted. His gaze was unblinking. "Do I have a choice?"

Her fingers let go of the zipper pull. "Yes," she said slowly and turned to face him. "Nobody is trying to run your life for you, Mason." She didn't know what was more disturbing. His presence, the taste of his name on her lips after all this time or the disturbing notion that he considered himself some sort of captive.

"You'll be the first nurse who hasn't tried."

She leaned her hip against the dresser and folded her arms over her chest. In just the one night that they'd shared, he'd learned her body better than she'd known it herself. But other than the fact that he worked for the same company that had nearly stolen her brother for good, what she really knew about Mason could have fit on the head of a pin.

"Then I'll be the first," she said quietly. "The only thing I'm doing here is making sure you continue your recovery safely and with as much comfort as possible. You're the one in control of your situation. Not me."

His eyes narrowed slightly, which just seemed to concentrate that pale green and make it even more startling against his dark lashes. "Why did you agree to all this?" He lifted his hand, taking in the room and, she presumed, the situation in general.

She chewed the inside of her lip, then went for honesty. "I didn't know you were the patient," she admitted. "Not until after I'd agreed."

He lifted his eyebrow. "Why didn't you back out?"

Now, that was trickier.

She shrugged. "I don't know." She did, but she had no intention of sharing her reasoning.

Remember what you're doing this for.

"So." She patted the duffel bag. "Do you want me to leave this for you to deal with…or…?"

He was silent for so long that she couldn't help wondering even more what was inside his head. She'd wondered a whole lot that night they'd been together, too. At least, she had during the moments when she'd been able to draw a coherent breath.

Which had been few and far between.

She swallowed down the jangling memory.

"Knock yourself out," he finally said.

Feeling ridiculously relieved to have something to keep her hands busy, she turned to the task. He had a few pairs of jeans, a half-dozen colored T-shirts and a handful of sweatpants—all one-legged like the pair he was wearing. The sum total of his clothing wasn't enough to fill even two of the six dresser drawers, and the pair of athletic shoes and scuffed cowboy boots didn't come close to filling the floor of the bedroom closet.

Aside from a small leather shaving kit, the rest of the duffel was crammed with books, which explained the weight.

Hardbacks. Paperbacks. Some that looked brand new and others that looked as if they'd seen the wear from hundreds of hands. She stacked a bunch of books on the nightstand next to the bed, where they'd be in easy reach for him. "You're a reader." And an eclectic reader, to boot. He had everything from the latest thriller topping the bestseller charts to political commentaries and biographies to classic literature.

He shifted against the pillows, and she couldn't help but see the way a thin line of white formed around his tightly held lips. "So?"

She adjusted the high stack. "Don't get defensive. It's just an observation." She left the rest of the books in a stack on the dresser. "And not that it looks like you'll run through all of these anytime soon, but I have a pretty loaded bookcase myself in the living room, too. You're welcome to help yourself. Do you prefer to get around with wheels or these?" She held up the crutches.

"Those," he said immediately. "Get rid of the chair altogether."

"All right." She propped the crutches right next to the bed, between the headboard and the nightstand. "Besides the books, feel free to help yourself to anything else around here."

He lifted his eyebrow again, giving her a long look, and she pressed her lips together. He was toying with her. "Food-wise and such," she clarified. "I'll get you set up with a meal before I have to go to the hospital for my shift and bring Plato in so you can meet him. He's gotten spoiled and used to having this bed for his own, but he's a smart boy. You just tell him to stay off and he will."

"Plato?"

She realized she was speaking so fast she was almost babbling and hated giving him any evidence that she was unsettled by his presence. "My Saint Bernard. He's out in the backyard right now."

"You didn't have a dog before."

"I didn't own a house with a yard before," she returned.

"No." His gaze felt heavy on her face. "You had that apartment."

Her throat suddenly felt dry and she swallowed, folding her arms over her chest. His gaze seemed to focus on them. Or on the achingly tight breasts that they were pressing against.

Probably her imagination.

Hopefully, just her imagination.

It was difficult enough ignoring her attraction for him, without thinking that he still carried some for her, too.

"What, um, what do you like to eat?"

His eyebrow peaked.

"For lunch," she added doggedly.

"There's nothing that I don't much like."

She moistened her lips. "You're not exactly helping me here, Mason. If I came in here with brussels sprouts, would you be loving them?"

His expression suddenly lightened, and a faint smile toyed around his surprisingly lush lower lip. "Honey, as long as I don't have to cook 'em, I'll be damn happy to eat 'em."

She exhaled and rolled her eyes. "Spoken like most men," she said wryly and headed out of the bedroom, taking the wheelchair with her.

She didn't breathe again, though, until she reached the privacy of the kitchen, and once she did, it took considerable effort not to collapse on a chair and just sit there.

But she hadn't been exaggerating to Mason. She did have to get to work soon.

Just because her bank account was going to be dancing a jig before this was all over and Mason went on his way in a few months, didn't mean that she didn't have to earn her regular wages.

She folded the chair and stowed it in a closet, then moved past the ladder-back chairs surrounding the kitchen table that was tucked into the small bay overlooking her backyard, and pulled open the refrigerator door. Until recently, she'd never made much effort at cooking for herself. She'd never had to. It was always so easy just to drop by her folks' place, or one of her other relatives', and grab a bite when she was looking for some home-cooked food.

But things were changing. Takeout and scavenged meals weren't going to do. So, after she'd moved into the house, she'd begun making an effort, and now her refrigerator was well stocked with fresh fruits and vegetables.

She had a chicken casserole that she'd made the day before, as well as sliced pot roast, and she chose the thick, sliced beef to make two sandwiches for Mason. She added a sliced apple, a glass of water and a thick wedge of peach pie that she couldn't take credit for since Ryan had brought it over.

Not giving herself a moment to dither over the meal— and dither she would, if she allowed it—she arranged everything on a sturdy wooden tray and carried it back to the bedroom, stopping only long enough to grab up the envelope with his meds and tuck it under her arm.

She breezed into the bedroom, her footsteps hesitating when she found him with his nose in a book, a pair of black-rimmed glasses perched almost incongruously on his aquiline nose.

Why she found the sight so particularly touching, she couldn't say. But she did. Which just meant that she had to push a brisk tone past the tightness in her chest. "I have soda or iced tea, if you want something to drink other than water." She tossed the envelope on the foot of the bed and grabbed the well-used folding lap table that she'd already had on hand and deftly set it over his lap, sliding the tray on top of it. "Or beer," she added, remembering that had been his preference before. "Though, you really shouldn't have alcohol right now."

She glanced at him, waiting, and found him watching her, his glasses and book set aside. "What?" she asked.

"How'd you do that without spilling the water?"

Surprised, she looked down at the lap tray and meal. "Practice," she said simply. "So…what do you want to drink besides water?"

His gaze passed her to land on the envelope lying near his foot. His lips tightened a little and he looked back at the meal. "Water's all I need." His jaw slid slightly to one side, then centered again. "Thank you. This looks good. I was half-afraid you'd be bringing in brussels sprouts."

She smiled slightly. "Behave yourself and I won't have to." She picked up the envelope and poured the bottles out into her hand. "When was your last dose of antibiotics?"

He didn't look up from the food. "Before I left Connecticut."

Which meant too many hours. She set all but two of the bottles on the nightstand, where they'd be in easy reach for him, and poured out his doses, setting them on the tray. "You missed a dose."

"I'll live."

"What's your pain like?"

He bit off a huge corner of thick-sliced bread and tender beef and shrugged.

Macho men.

"On a scale of one to five," she prodded. "Five being the worst."

"Twelve," he muttered around his mouthful.

She wasn't particularly surprised. She could practically see his discomfort oozing out of his pores. "Good thing you're eating," she said and popped the lid off his painkillers. "It'll help keep your stomach settled with this stuff."

He lifted his hand, stopping her before she could drop one on her palm. "Throw the damn things down the toilet. I don't need 'em."

She gave him a look. *"Twelve?"*

His gaze slid over hers, then away. "Fine." His voice was short. "I don't want them."

"It's not a sign of weakness to need—"

"I *said* no."

She slowly put the cap back on the bottle, sensing that this was about something other than macho posturing. And, judging by the way he was holding himself even more stiffly than before, that he didn't want her prying.

Which told her more than words could have said, anyway.

"Fair enough." She set the bottle next to the others. "But you don't have a choice about those," she said firmly. She pointed to the two pills next to his plate. "If you want your bones to heal, you've got to beat back that infection once and for all." She headed to the doorway. "I'll go get Plato."

Mason watched Courtney stride out of the room.

It was a helluva thing that he was almost more interested in the damn pill bottle within arm's reach than he was in watching the particularly enjoyable sight of her shapely form moving underneath the thin pink fabric of her scrubs.

He swallowed the last of the first sandwich, leaned his head back against the pillows and closed his eyes. Too easily, the night they'd spent together came to life in his mind.

He pinched the bridge of his nose and opened his eyes again.

Since the moment he'd thrown McDougal's daughter, Lari, to safety, he'd been in hell.

Coming to Weaver was just one more layer of it.

There was no future for Courtney with him, and she was the kind of woman who deserved futures. She was young and beautiful and caring and came from a strong, close family.

He was past young, scarred on the inside as well as

the out, and the only family he knew—or who mattered to him—was the family of Hollins-Winword.

It was a fact of life that was easy enough to remember when he was a continent or two away from her.

But sprawled across a bed under her *roof?*

That was an entirely different matter.

"Plato, come meet Mason."

He heard her voice before her footsteps and then she reappeared in the doorway with a gigantic Saint Bernard at her side.

"You didn't get a dog." Mason eyed the shaggy beast. "You got a damn horse."

She grinned, bringing a surprising impishness to her oval face, and tucked her long, golden hair behind her ear. "He's a big boy," she agreed. Her fingers scrubbed through the dog's thick coat and the beast's tongue lolled with obvious pleasure. "But he's a total marshmallow. He's four and very well behaved." She stopped next to the bed and gestured to the dog, who plopped his butt on the floor and looked across the mattress at Mason with solemn brown eyes. "Mason's a friend, Plato."

Mason stuck out his good hand and let the dog sniff him. Evidently satisfied, the dog slopped his tongue over Mason's fingers and thumped his tail a few times.

Courtney smiled, then looked at the watch around her wrist. "I've got to get to work." Her gaze skipped over Mason and around the room. She picked up the cell phone that Axel had left. "I'm adding the number at the hospital," she said as her fingers rapidly tapped. "Plus my own cell number." When she was finished, she set the phone on the nightstand. "But I'll warn you—cell service isn't always the greatest around here. There's a landline in the kitchen, though." She patted her hip. "Come on, Plato. Back outside."

"Does he always stay outside?"

Courtney shook her head. "Not always. But I don't want him disturbing you."

Mason leaned forward a little, rubbing his hand over the dog's massive head. "He'll give me someone to talk to."

She smiled slightly. "Well. He is pretty good company. I'll pop back home when I get my dinner break, but it'll be pretty late." She headed toward the doorway. "Don't hesitate to call if you need anything, though. If I can't make it over, there's always going to be someone who can." She gave a faint wave and disappeared.

Mason looked from the doorway to the pill bottles on the bedside table to the dog, who was watching him as if he could read his mind.

"Don't you worry, Plato," Mason muttered. "Soon as I get these casts off, I'll be out of here."

And away from temptation.

He looked from the prescription bottle back to the empty doorway.

Both temptations.

"It sounds like the perfect opportunity for you." Lisa Pope, the other nurse who shared the emergency room's night shift with Courtney, leaned her elbows on the counter and smiled. "Keep an eye out for a patient while he heals up *and* collect room and board at the same time."

Courtney didn't look up from the medical chart she was updating and smiled a little wryly. "It does sound perfect," she agreed. In theory.

"*Sounds* perfect," Lisa prompted. She raised her eyebrows. "What's the problem?"

Courtney shook her head. "No problem." None that she intended to share.

Lisa leaned closer over the desk. At the moment, the Weaver Hospital's emergency department was quiet. "He must not have a wife, or he wouldn't need care. So is he handsome?" Her eyes danced wickedly.

"Whether he is or not is beside the point. He's a *patient.*"

Lisa sighed noisily and straightened. "Honestly, girl. You are twenty-six years old, so beautiful that other women ought to hate you, and I swear you live the life of a nun. It's practically criminal."

Courtney gave a laughing snort. "Why does it matter to you? You're besotted with your husband, and you know it." Lisa and Jay even had a darling little girl, Annie.

Lisa lifted her shoulder. "Maybe so, but that doesn't mean a little vicarious living is out of the question. So... handsome or not?"

Courtney gave a huge sigh and closed the chart. "Mason is—" She broke off, trying to find a good word to describe the man and failing entirely. "Handsome enough." She settled on the adjective, just because it was expedient. Despite the scar on his face, he was a striking man. Not handsome exactly, because he had a certain aura of...darkness around him. "More importantly, he's a *patient.*"

Lisa made a face. "Well. At least tell me you're going to spend the extra money you're earning on something more interesting than fresh paint for your house trim. For nine months, all you've talked about is that house of yours."

A laugh started to bubble in the back of Courtney's throat.

Nine months.

It was almost funny.

She looked across the counter at her coworker and friend and shrugged casually, hiding the squiggle of excitement inside her. "What can I say? It's my home. I want it to be perfect."

Perfect for when it wasn't just her living there.

Then she waved her hands in a shooing motion as she turned her attention back to paperwork that needed to be completed ASAP. "Now, we'd better get back to work or the boss lady around this place will have our heads."

They both grinned, because the boss lady who ran the Weaver Hospital happened to be Courtney's mother, Dr. Rebecca Clay. But the grins didn't last long because the doors to the E.R. slid open, and Courtney's sister-in-law, Mallory, strode inside, shrugging out of her jacket as she moved. "Got a high-risk mom coming in by air," she greeted as she moved rapidly across the tiled floor past the desk where Courtney and Lisa were. "They're at least ten minutes out."

Courtney was already following her. "I'll call the team." She didn't even look back to see Lisa assume her seat at reception.

Mallory nodded and pushed through the double doors, Courtney on her heels.

The quiet evening was over, and Courtney didn't have a chance to think about much of anything until it was time for her dinner break at ten o'clock.

She drove the short distance home and let herself into the house. There was a water glass sitting on the counter in the kitchen where she hadn't left it, but that was the only indication that Mason had been moving around the house.

A light came from his room down the hall, and she headed there quietly in case he was sleeping. She stuck her head around the doorway and looked inside.

He was sprawled on the bed, more or less in the same position that she'd left him. A book was lying closed on the mattress beside him, and Plato was lying next to that.

Her dog's brow wrinkled as he looked at her, but he didn't lift his head. He looked as if he were settled for the night. Between the big dog and the big man, there was barely a spare inch of mattress left.

Courtney settled a light blanket over Mason and turned off the light. Mason still didn't stir. That was good. He needed sleep.

"Good boy," she whispered to Plato, giving his head a scratch.

She left the house again and went back to the hospital to finish her shift. The second half passed even more quickly than the first, thanks to a motorcycle accident on the highway outside of town. It was just after three o'clock when she got home again.

Mason's room was still quiet, except for the faint sound of his snoring.

She smiled a little to herself and went into her own bedroom, which was across the hall from his. She exchanged her scrubs for a pair of lightweight pajama pants and a tank and then—because she always needed to unwind for a while after getting off shift—headed out to the family room again. She'd barely sat down in front of her computer when she heard the pad of Plato's paws. He propped his head on her knee, flopping his tail against the floor.

"So, Plato. Are you ready to have a baby?"

Chapter Three

Courtney rested her chin on her palm and stared at the computer screen, her mind eagerly whisking into the future.

"A little boy or a little girl?" She didn't care which. She glanced at the dog. "Come this time next year, we'll have a smiling, gurgling little someone to cuddle. What do you think?"

Plato's warm brown eyes stared back at her. He made a low sound that she took as complete agreement.

Brilliant dog that he was.

She grinned and reached out to run her fingers through his thick, silky hair, and he grinned back at her, pushing his head harder against her palm. His long, feathered tail slapped the base of her chair. "I knew you'd like the idea, too." Plato had been around children before she'd adopted him. His previous owner had run a foster home before cancer had stricken her.

Thinking of the woman who hadn't only been Courtney's teacher in Cheyenne, but also her friend, made her sigh.

Then she leaned over and pressed a kiss on Plato's big head before turning back to the computer screen that glowed in front of her. She wasn't going to end up like Margaret, taking in other people's children when they couldn't properly care for them. For Margaret, that had been enough.

Not for Courtney.

She wanted a child of her own.

"Thank goodness for Axel, huh?" She didn't look away from the computer screen. "If it weren't for him, we'd be waiting even longer." Of course, when her cousin had approached her about taking in Mason, he'd had no idea of her plans and still didn't. For that matter, nobody in her family had any idea.

She simply wasn't ready to share, yet.

She looked back at her faithful companion and scrubbed her fingers through his thick coat again. "You're the only one who knows," she whispered.

The four-year-old Saint Bernard gave a huge, contented sigh.

Which had pretty much been the dog's reaction ever since she'd begun voicing her intention to add to their small family.

She was twenty-six years old. Financially independent in a modest way. She had a good job. She—along with the bank—owned a home that she'd spent the past nine months remodeling.

And she wanted a baby.

So what if she didn't have a man in her life?

Weaver, Wyoming, was a small town. She'd known all of the available men here since they'd all pretty much been in diapers. She also knew the men who weren't available, yet liked to think they were.

She had no problem giving them *all* a pass.

The fact was, not a single man in Weaver had ever really turned her head, romantically speaking.

Well.

She grimaced slightly. Not any man who was *from* Weaver, she amended, thinking of the man sleeping right down the hall from her.

She was a modern, independent woman.

She had scads of supportive—albeit nosy—family members in the area. Everything in her life was aligned perfectly, just as she'd planned and worked for.

And now, thanks to Axel's suggestion and Mason's rent, she'd have the funds she needed even sooner than she'd planned.

If she'd learned anything in her life, it was not to wait too long to put into action the things you wanted.

Well, the waiting was done.

For months, she'd been checking out the various websites of sperm banks. Checking references. Checking reputations. And she'd finally settled on one—Big Sky Cryobank. It was located in Montana, had been around for as long as she'd been alive and came with impeccable references.

Now, given what she was earning, thanks to Mason, she would be able to bank enough extra money to pay the cryobank fees and the associated physician fees, since she knew her health insurance wasn't going to cover the process of *getting* pregnant. She'd also have enough in her savings to tide her over for a few months when the baby came, so she wouldn't have to go back to work the very second her maternity leave was used up.

"Everything is perfect," she told Plato.

The dog stared up at her as if he could read her mind.

She grimaced a little. All right. Modern, independent woman or not, she had to admit that "perfect" *would* be the husband and a wedding ring along with the baby she was desperate to have. But she wasn't willing to wait for all of that to come knocking at her door. Not when her door—save that one night with Mason all those months ago—was essentially silent. "As perfect as it's likely to get," she allowed, giving Plato a firm look.

"What's perfect?"

She jerked, her heart lurching in her chest, and spun around on her chair to peer down the darkened hallway. "Mason. What are you doing awake?"

His rubber-tipped crutches provided a slow, rhythmic clump as he moved closer.

Her heart hadn't stopped lurching, and she rose, wishing like fury that she'd thought to put on a robe over her thin knit pajamas. Thank heavens the room was lit only by a small lamp and the glow from her computer monitor. He would never be able to see the thumping in her chest, which felt so heavy it was probably visible. "I hope I didn't wake you."

He finally stopped on the other side of the dining room table. He shook his head.

She moistened her lips and pressed her palms down the sides of her drawstring pants. "Do you need anything? You were sleeping when I came by during my break, and I didn't want to disturb you then. But if you're hungry or thirsty, I'm happy to get something for you." Better to have a task to focus on, even if she did realize that she was talking too fast in the process.

He shook his head again, then jerked his chin toward the computer. "What's that? One of those computer dating websites? Searching for your perfect match?"

She barely kept herself from shutting off the computer monitor. "Sort of."

His dark gaze shifted back to her. "What're you looking for? Blond hair? Dark hair? Blue eyes? Brown?"

She laughed a little nervously. Maybe if she described him, he'd drop the subject. Or not, considering his "sex option" comment when he'd arrived.

She wasn't brave enough to find out.

Nor was she brave enough to hear what sort of comments he might have about her decision to find a daddy for her baby through a sperm bank. She pushed a few buttons on the computer keyboard, and the screen went blank, and she moved toward him. Away from the narrow desk where the computer sat. But the closer she got to him, the warmer she became.

Fortunately, there were a few working brain cells left inside her head for her to realize the heat wasn't coming from inside her, but physically radiating from him. At a temperature much higher than normal.

She reached up and pressed her palm against his forehead. He was burning up.

"Mason," she tsked. "You have a fever. Are you in pain?"

"No." He'd closed his eyes and sighed faintly when she'd laid her hand on his forehead. The kind of sigh that signaled relief.

"I don't believe you," she murmured, but left her hand on his forehead a moment longer than necessary before she tucked herself between his casted arm and his side. She slid the crutch out of her way and leaned it against the table.

The feel of his torso against hers was blazing hot.

"Come on. You shouldn't be on your feet." She

wrapped her arm behind his back for support and gently nudged him in the direction of the hallway.

"I don't want to go back to bed. I'm sick of beds at the moment."

"Okay." She shifted slightly. "How about the couch?"

He gave a faint grunt and, with most of his weight on his remaining crutch, headed toward it. By the time he'd managed to half hop and half crutch his way around until he could pretty much collapse on the smooth leather cushions, she was glad she'd rearranged the furniture. She was also out of breath, and she didn't consider herself exactly out of shape. Not with the running that she did.

She propped her hands on her hips and blew out a breath. "Now stay there."

"Funny girl." He finally let go of the crutch that he was still clutching, and it slid to the floor. "I hate this," he muttered.

A fresh wave of sympathy plowed over her. "I can only imagine." She gently shushed Plato out of the way when he tried tucking his big head on the couch next to Mason, then grabbed one of the soft throw pillows from the opposite end of the couch and deftly tucked it behind his head. "Just take a few deep breaths. I'll be right back." The dog trotted after her as she hurried into Mason's bedroom. He gave her a faint woof, then leapt up onto the bed, turned around a few times and lay down.

Courtney left him there, retrieved the wedge cushion, as well as Mason's antibiotics, grabbed a bottled water from the refrigerator in her kitchen and wet down a clean washcloth.

She went back to him and folded the damp cloth over his forehead.

He lifted his hand to it. "I don't need that."

She pushed it right back into place. "This is not coddling," she assured drily.

"Feels like it."

"Stop complaining." She rattled the antibiotics bottle. "Did you take a dose before you went to sleep?"

"Yes, Nurse Ratched."

She couldn't help but grin. The big, tall, dangerous-looking man sounded as cranky as an overtired five-year-old. "Mason, you have no idea," she warned lightly. "I work the night shift in an emergency room. I can order the meanest sons of guns around."

"I'm shaking in my boots."

"You're not wearing any," she reminded him, then went to her own medicine cabinet in her bathroom to retrieve a bottle of acetaminophen as well as her ear thermometer.

Back in the living room, she spotted the wet cloth clutched in his fist and not on his forehead.

Stubborn.

But then, so was she.

She shook out a few of the pills, opened the bottle of water and tugged the damp cloth of out his grip, then handed them to him.

"What are they?"

"Good old Tylenol. For fever and maybe to help dull the pain a little." She didn't think now was the best time to broach the subject of his prescribed painkillers. He'd already said he refused to take them, and that was his right.

He swallowed the pills and drank down half the bottle of water, then leaned his head back again against the square pillow. She folded the cloth once more over his forehead. "Leave it." She touched his chin lightly and tried to ignore the tantalizing feel of that raspy chin. "Turn your head a little."

"Why?" His voice dripped with suspicion.

"So I can torture you some more, of course." She held up her thermometer. "I need your ear for a moment."

He grimaced and turned his head slightly.

"Take comfort in the fact that it could be worse." She quickly took his temp and then sat back on her heels. "Well, it's not as high as I thought it might be, but if it's not back down to normal by morning, I'm going to have my mother come by."

He pulled the cloth off his face and gave her a look. "Your mother."

"She's a doctor."

He shook his head slightly. "Right. I should have remembered that."

She tugged the cloth out of his hand yet again and replaced it on his forehead. "Should? Why?"

"I met her once," he said, sounding annoyed. "Because I remember stuff. I'm supposed to remember stuff."

She didn't know why she was unnerved to think that he'd met her mother. He'd spent a few weeks in Weaver around the time that they'd been…uninvolved. It wasn't unnatural to think he might have met more of her family than just *her,* particularly since he'd been working with Axel. "Stuff…about cases?"

He lifted the cloth enough to give her a baleful look from beneath it. "Cases of what?"

Fortunately, she had a lifetime of experience dealing with men who thought they could control a situation with just such a look. "Cases for the agency, naturally."

Mason felt only slightly better than roadkill, yet he

still was shocked by the words that Courtney uttered so blithely. "What do you know about the agency?"

"More than I ever wanted to," she assured evenly. "We nearly lost my brother because of Hollins-Winword. You work for them, too." Her gaze drifted over him.

Maybe he did have a fever, because it felt like everywhere that amber gaze landed, a fire started to burn. "I never told you about my work." He damn sure had never mentioned the name of the agency.

"So you *don't* work for them? And I'll bet the fact that you're laid up like this has nothing to do with them, either." She was still crouched on the floor beside the couch. It was a physical effort to drag his eyes away from the warm, golden glow of her.

So much skin, and so much on display, thanks to the thin shirt that she wore.

His fingers twitched, and he pushed around the cloth on his forehead just to keep them busy. "Right now I'm not working for anybody." It was true enough in a sense. But since he was more or less toeing the line that Cole had drawn in the sand, it was only a temporary truth. "And I'm laid up because I wasn't moving fast enough when I needed to."

"Mmm." She didn't look convinced.

He wasn't in the mood to argue about it. For one thing, it wouldn't serve any good purpose.

All he needed to remember was that she was his landlady for the time being. A landlady nurse.

Who smelled like something soft and powdery and gently alluring.

She moved and her hand nudged his, slipping the cloth away. "I'll get this wet again for you."

He didn't argue that, either, and watched her straighten and move across the living area, around the small dining table that shared the space with her computer and through an arch that led to the kitchen.

Her long hair swayed against her slender back that was faithfully outlined by her thin blue tank top. And then there was the womanly flare of her hips and the long, long legs. ...

Watching her was like watching a fantasy unroll in his head.

Only, the night that they'd spent together had been indelibly real, and he knew good and well that the reality was eons better than any fantasy.

He heard the sound of water and then she was walking back toward him, and the front view was equally as magnificent as the rear view had been.

He wondered who had been living the fantasy with her lately and grimaced over the acid taste that thought put in his mouth. "Why *are* you trolling the internet for matches?"

Her smooth, stupefyingly feminine walk halted. She blinked once, then shrugged casually. "Why does anyone? Because they're curious? Bored?" She crossed the last few steps to the couch and lowered the blessedly cool cloth to his forehead again. "Lonely? Hopeful?"

"I'm not asking about anyone." A yawn suddenly split his face. "Sorry," he muttered and tried to shift, but the cast on his leg made it awkward, and the sharp pain in his back made it impossible. He bit back an oath. "I'm asking about *you.*"

She was watching him with that sympathetic, "poor baby" look in her eyes. "I guess you could put me in the hopeful camp," she said after a moment.

"So you're trying to find yourself a husband. On the damn internet. Don't you know the dangers there are in—"

"Don't you know that I'm a grown woman and am

more than capable of handling any supposed dangers out there? How's it any worse than meeting a stranger in a bar? Or a Valentine's Day kissing booth?" she added with pointed amusement. "And just to be clear, I am *not* looking for a husband."

"Just to be clear," he returned, "I know you're a grown woman. My memory's not impaired about that, at all."

She cleared her throat, her amusement seeming to dissipate in the blink of an eye. "I think it would be better if we just pretended that never happened."

His head was throbbing. His toes sticking out from the bottom of his cast were throbbing. And every spot in between was throbbing. He felt like he was burning from the inside out, and not all of it was because of some stupid temperature.

The fever he had for her was ninety percent of his problem.

"You brought it up first," he reminded. "But if you can pretend, go for it. I can't."

"Why *not?*" For the first time, he heard frustration in her voice. "It was just one night."

"Yeah, it was one night. But there wasn't anything *just* about it."

She shook her head. It only made the long, thick strands of gold hair slide across her gold shoulder and curl over the full jut of her breast, which was clearly— thank you, Lord, for torturing him with that incredible sight—delineated by the thin fabric of her shirt.

"It's only going to make things…awkward," she insisted.

"Then things will be awkward," he said flatly. "'Cause I can't forget about it." Nor did he want to.

The night they'd spent together was as much a perfect memory as it was a very necessary reminder.

Making love with her had been the most indescribable thing he'd ever experienced. And he needed to remember that it had been *temporary.*

Short-lived by necessity.

And by choice.

He pressed the damp, not-so-cool cloth down over his eyes. "Just make sure you're careful about it." His voice sounded as dark as he felt inside. "Meeting up with whatever *hopeful* suitors you find. There're a lot of crazies out there. And guys who'll take advantage of you the second you let down your guard."

"So...you don't have any problem with the idea of me finding a, um, a date like this." Her voice went so smooth that warning bells jangled in the back of his mind.

She sounded miffed.

If he were honest, he could have told her, hell yeah, he had a problem with it.

He had a problem with the notion of her going out with any other guy, no matter where or how she met the man.

He had a problem thinking about anyone touching her. Physically. Emotionally.

But that sort of honesty wouldn't get them anywhere.

"Like you said. You're a grown woman. It would be unusual if you didn't want to date." To marry. Have children. "Though, I'd have thought you'd have plenty of pickings at the hospital and wouldn't have to *resort* to meeting strangers in a bar. Or aren't there any eligible doctors there?"

She was silent just long enough that his curiosity started nagging at him and he peered at her from beneath the cloth again. She was chewing at the inside of her lip, her eyes narrowed. But after a moment, all she said was, "You should be in bed."

"No."

He was almost surprised when she didn't argue.

"All right. But if you need to get up or anything, just call my name. I'll hear you."

The last damn thing he wanted to do was call her name so she could help his sorry butt off the couch just so he could take a leak. That was the only thing he could think of at the moment that would make him willing enough to bring on a fresh set of agony by moving around.

Unless it was to go to *her* bed.

Which would be a joke right now.

The mind and some parts of his body were definitely willing, but the rest of him—the injured, aching part of him—just sat back with a snide, cruel laugh at the very idea of it.

"I'll yell," he said, having no intentions of it at all. "G'night."

She hesitated a moment longer, still looking strangely indecisive. But then she did turn on her heel and head down the hall. A moment later, he heard the sound of a door closing softly. Then water running.

His fertile mind took off like a shot, and again, the part of him that was in control got a damn good laugh.

His head hurt. His ribs and his back hurt. He had an itch beneath the cast on his arm that was driving him batty. It was hours before he finally dozed off. The sky that he could see through a kitchen window was beginning to lighten. And when he did sleep, his dreams were a jumbled mess.

Cole was behind the wheel of the SUV aiming for little Lari McDougal. Mason watched it all unfold, his dream-state legs refusing to run fast enough, knowing he wasn't going to make it. Wasn't going to be able to save the child.

Only, Lari wasn't a child, he realized as he forced his legs to move through the sludgelike paralysis that was holding him in place. It was Courtney.

Beautiful, young Courtney.

The SUV was speeding closer. Mason could see the whites of Coleman Black's eyes.

He yelled out to Lari. To Courtney.

Knew it was too late. He was too late....

He jerked and barely caught himself from rolling off the couch. His heart was pounding in his chest, his breath coming fast and hard.

But at least he knew where he was.

In Courtney's house. Sleeping on a surprisingly un-comfortable leather couch while cool sunshine streamed through the plentiful windows.

The washcloth was still damp but annoyingly so, con-sidering it was caught under his neck.

Grabbing the back of the couch with his good hand, he managed to pull himself up until he was sitting, and then he worked on getting his bulky, casted leg out of his way long enough so he could get his butt up and off the couch.

There was no sound from the bedrooms, and he was glad to think that she was still sleeping, since he didn't relish the idea of Courtney witnessing his fumbling struggles just to get onto his feet.

She'd left his crutches propped against the chair and, balancing on his good leg, he leaned over to grab them. Only, as he did so, something in his back grabbed with talon sharpness and before he knew it, he was off bal-ance and crashing face-first on the floor.

"Dammit!" Pain ricocheted through every corner, and he rolled onto his back, staring up at the ceiling.

It was crisscrossed with rough-hewn beams.

"Mason?" He heard her running, and then she was in the room with him, her knees grazing his good arm as she knelt down, her hands fluttering over him. She pressed her palm to his forehead. "Fever's gone. What on earth were you doing?"

She smelled warm. Bed warm. Sweet warm.

And his hankering for that sweetness was heading straight off the charts.

Which was not a helpful thing at the moment.

She peered into his face. "Are you hurt?"

"Besides my pride?" He tried using his hands to push himself up, only to swear and fall back on the floor at the searing pain that shot through his arm. His teeth came together as he swore again.

"Don't try to move anymore." Now she was leaning over him, and every centimeter of him—despite the nagging pain in his back—homed in on the soft push of her full breasts against his chest. Only when she was slipping her arm beneath his shoulder and neck did he realize she'd been reaching for the throw pillow.

Which she tucked beneath his head.

Then she pushed to her feet and stepped right over his body, jogging into the kitchen. She was back in seconds, with a phone at her ear.

"I'm *not* going back to the hospital," he warned flatly.

Even if it meant he was going to shrivel up and rot right there on her living room floor, he wasn't moving.

"You *are,*" she returned just as flatly. "Your cast looks like it's cracked."

He automatically started to raise his arm to look for himself, but a sharp pang warned him to stop.

He muttered another oath.

"Thanks. We'll be waiting," Courtney was saying into the phone before she set it down on the table.

"Waiting for who?"

"Not an ambulance," she said, "so you can stop worrying about that."

Getting carted away in an ambulance wasn't the worst of his worries, but it wasn't something he necessarily wanted. "Then, again, waiting for whom?"

"Axel. I want some help before I get you off the floor. Plus, you'll be able to ride much more comfortably in the front seat of his steroid-size pickup truck than you would in my little economy job." She stood near his bare feet, her hands propped on her hips. Her hair was sleep tousled and tangled around her shoulders, and the pajamas that had looked thin in the middle of the night looked even thinner during the cold light of morning.

He wished he could lie there and just look at her for a long, long while.

"I'm not going to *stay* at the hospital," he warned. "They can fix the cast. But I'm not going to stay."

She tilted her head slightly and a thick lock of long blond hair curled alongside the jut of her breast. "What is it with you and hospitals? Just dislike on general principle, or are you afraid you won't be in control there, and you'll end up with some of these in your system?" She pulled something out of the hidden pocket in her thin pants and held it up.

It was the bottle of pain pills that he'd dumped in the trash while she'd been at work.

He had actually opened the bottle and poured two pills out on his shaking palm before his better sense had forced him to return them to the bottle and pitch it in the trash.

Chapter Four

Courtney knew she was skirting close to the truth when Mason's gaze flickered.

Then he narrowed his eyes, and his expression became unreadable. "Wouldn't have pegged you for someone who likes to dig in the trash."

"Since you didn't work very hard to get rid of it, it wasn't hard to find." The bottle had been the only thing lying at the bottom of the small, decorative waste bin in the hallway bathroom. It would have been pretty hard *not* to notice it. She also noticed that he hadn't emptied the bottle's contents down the drain, which told her that he didn't want them around but wasn't quite ready to make it a reality.

If she could pluck the bottle out of the waste bin—narcotic contents no worse for the wear—then so could he.

She set the pills on the table next to the telephone. If Axel was true to his word, he'd be there any second, and she needed to get some real clothes on—or at least a fresh pair of scrubs—before they went to the hospital. She didn't really want to parade around in front of her coworkers in her jammies.

Nevertheless, she pulled out one of the dining room table chairs, turned it around and sat where Mason could see her with no effort. She folded her arms across her knees and leaned forward. "I'm guessing you had a dependency problem?"

His expression went even more blank.

"You don't have to tell me all the details. Or any of them, unless you choose to. But it would be helpful where your *care* is concerned to know if it's something recent or not."

His scar, where it traveled over his temple, looked white. Whiter, even, than the line around his thinly compressed lips. "Not." The word was snapped off.

It was more of an answer than she'd expected to get.

The woman inside had a million questions that she had to squelch. The nurse, though, had only a few. "Would it be better for you if I really did flush 'em?"

"No, because I could get more if I wanted."

She knew that was true enough. "Are you going to want to?"

His lashes lifted. The green of his eyes was pale. Sharp. "That remains to be seen, doesn't it?"

His honesty felt brutal. During her nursing training in Cheyenne, she'd volunteered at a detoxification and rehabilitation unit. She'd worked with patients of all ages, both sexes, those who came from money and those who were living on the streets. Some were there by choice and some weren't. She'd heard every story, every excuse, every reason for how and why they were there in the first place, every reason and every goal for how and why they wouldn't be back.

Some made it through. Some didn't.

Those who were the most successful were the ones who were honest—with themselves, at least—through every step they took.

"Well." Her voice sounded husky, even to her own ears. "Try to remember that it isn't a crime to ask for help when you need it. And that's what I'm here for. To help you until you're back on your feet."

"The only help I need at the moment is for you to sit up, so I can't see straight down that excuse of a shirt you're wearing right to the little pink jewel stud in your navel."

She sat bolt upright. She hadn't had her navel pierced when they'd slept together. Getting their navels pierced was one of the last things she and Margaret had done together.

"Sorry." Even as she said the word, she felt heat fill her cheeks.

"I'm not. Most entertaining thing that's happened to me since I planted my face on your floor."

"Which you wouldn't have done," she reminded him, "if you'd asked for assistance." She turned on her bare heel and hurried back to her bedroom, stopping only long enough to put the dog out in the backyard with fresh food and water.

By the time she'd thrown her hair up in a clip and pulled on a long-sleeved T-shirt, a pair of cargo pants, and shoved her feet into sandals, Axel—and her brother, Ryan—had arrived.

"I stopped and picked up reinforcements," Axel told her when she stopped in surprise at the sight of her brother.

Between the two men, they had gotten Mason off the floor and onto his crutches.

"Hey, there." Courtney smiled at her brother. He'd been back in their lives now for over a year, but it still felt like a miracle every time she saw him. "How're the beautiful women in your life?"

"Beautiful." Ryan's lips tilted. "Mallory got called out early this morning on another emergency. Two in one night. I dropped Chloe off at school on my way here. When we left the house, Kathleen was trying to decide whether she wants to go out tonight with Fred Beeman— who is ten years younger than she is and can keep up with her during bowling, but lives with his daughter and granddaughter, thus cramping his style—or with Sam Driscoll, who is the same age as she is but still has all his own teeth, lives on his own and—honest to God, her words, not mine—has no need for that little blue pill." Ryan's blue gaze shifted to Mason. "Kathleen's my eighty-year-old grandmother-in-law," he told him and shook his head. "God help us all."

Courtney laughed. "We should all be so lucky to be filled with life the way Kathleen is." Goodness knew the woman had more romance in her life than Courtney did.

She realized her gaze had strayed to Mason at the thought and shook herself. "Glad they got you on your feet." She wasn't going to suggest she get the wheelchair that she'd folded up and stored in the closet. She'd told him where it was and, if he'd wanted to use it, she had no doubt that he would be sitting in it right now instead of standing there stiffly with his crutches, looking painfully uncomfortable. "Let's get that cast taken care of."

He didn't look enthusiastic, but he turned and slowly

crutched his way out of the house. When he got outside, she waited silently while he hesitated at the steps.

"For God's sake, Mase," Axel complained with the ease of friendship. "This would take half the time if you'd just plant your ass in that wheelchair you had."

Mason told Axel what he could do with his comment. Ryan rolled his eyes.

Courtney remained quiet. She might agree with the other men in theory, but Mason needed to feel like he had some control, even if it was just over the matter of trying to get out of her house.

He chose the stairs over the ramp and, even though it made her nearly bite off her tongue to keep from pointing out the pitfalls, she still said nothing. Instead, she walked down the ramp, leaving the men behind.

Between the two of them, her brother and Axel were more than capable of lending Mason some assistance if it became necessary, and she figured his pride would be better able to take it if she weren't watching.

So she climbed into the backseat of Axel's oversized pickup truck and watched the minute hand on her watch slowly tick along until finally, *finally,* Mason was inside the truck.

"The wheelchair would have been easier," he said under his breath, while Axel went around the front to the driver's side.

"Your choice," Courtney reminded.

Axel climbed behind the wheel, and Ryan drove off in his own truck, lightly tooting his horn as he went. "How the hell'd you end up on your butt, anyway?" Axel asked as he put the truck in motion, following Ryan down the quiet street.

"Trying to do too much," Courtney couldn't help answering with her own observation.

Mason just turned his head and stared out the side window, ignoring them both.

Fortunately, it took only a few minutes to reach the hospital. Axel pulled up right outside the emergency room entrance so that Mason wouldn't have to move far.

Courtney hopped out of the truck and went inside. She smiled at Wyatt Mead and Greer Weston, who were her counterparts on the day shift, while she grabbed one of the wheelchairs. "Call Richie in imaging and tell him to put down his book of Sudoku puzzles. Probably going to need him for a few minutes. And see if Dr. Jackman is around." He was the orthopedist on staff, and she'd copied him with Mason's records before he'd arrived in town.

"Jackman's not, but I saw Pierce Flannery on the floor a few minutes ago. Do you want me to flag him down before he leaves?"

She'd only met Dr. Flannery once. He had a private practice in Braden, with privileges at Weaver's hospital. After they'd met, she'd sidestepped his calls a few times, much to Lisa Pope's chagrin, who'd figured Courtney couldn't do much better than accept a date with the eligible doctor.

She would have preferred Dr. Jackman to look at Mason, but knew there was nothing wrong with Dr. Flannery except for the plain interest he'd shown in her. And her purpose there today was for Mason, anyway. So, she just nodded as she pushed the chair outside through the automatic sliding doors.

With Axel's help, Mason managed to move from the truck to the chair. "I'll come back and play taxi when you need me to, as long as it's not too late," Axel offered. "Tara and I are going down to Cheyenne for dinner tonight."

Courtney gave her cousin a quick look. "Cheyenne?"

He shrugged. "She wants to go to that bead store she likes to get some supplies for the jewelry she makes at the shop. Figured we might as well make an evening out of the drive. Right now, I've gotta run out to Tristan's office for a few minutes."

Tristan was Tristan Clay, one of their uncles, who owned CeeVid, a popular gaming company that was located in Weaver. Courtney didn't have proof, but she was pretty certain that CeeVid was also a cover for Hollins-Winword.

"I'll call when he's ready to get home," she told her cousin as she moved around the wheelchair. "Thanks."

"No prob," Axel assured as he headed around his truck again.

Courtney quickly adjusted the chair's footrest to support Mason's heavy cast and then pushed him inside. Scooping up the clipboard and forms that Wyatt was holding out, she deftly wheeled Mason around to roll backward through the swinging double doors that separated the waiting area from the exam area.

She knew it was a quiet morning by virtue of the empty beds in the exam area, and she positioned Mason's chair in the first "room"—which was really only an area that could be separated from the next bed by the long curtains that hung from U-shaped ceiling tracks. She retrieved a pen and handed it, along with the clipboard, to him.

He eyed the forms and exhaled roughly. "I don't have my reading glasses with me."

Remorse quickened. "I should have thought of them." If she didn't continually feel off balance around him, maybe she would have. "I'll fill it out for you." She took the board and the pen from him and commandeered one of the low, rolling stools for herself. She knew his first and last name, obviously, but that was pretty well it.

"Birthday?"

He told her and she filled in the squares, unable to hide her surprise. "Your birthday is February 15? The day after Valentine's Day?"

"So?"

She tucked her tongue in the roof of her mouth for a moment. "So…no reason." Just that they'd spent Valentine's night together in her bed. She guessed it was pretty plain why he hadn't thought to mention that it was his birthday the next day—because she hadn't mattered enough for him to share that fact. "I wouldn't have thought you were thirty-nine, though."

"Since I feel like I'm about sixty, I'm not sure how to take that."

She couldn't help but smile faintly. "You don't look older than your age," she assured mildly. In fact, despite his hard, scarred face and the few silver strands sprinkled in his dark hair, she thought he looked younger.

Thoughts which were not helping to get the necessary paperwork completed.

He gave her his home address in Connecticut, and when it came to his emergency contact, he shrugged. "None."

"Mason." She gave him a look. "You must have family. Someone."

"Coleman Black," he finally said with a sigh. "Close enough."

She'd met Coleman Black on more than one occasion. Not because she knew he was deeply involved in the agency that she was not supposed to know about, but because he was Brody Paine's father and Brody was married to her cousin Angeline.

Angeline, as far as Courtney had been able to discern, was much fonder of her father-in-law than Brody was.

"So you *are* with the agency," she murmured. He just gave her a stony look and she shook her head a little. "I don't see what the big secret is. Half my family has been involved with it or still are." She clicked the pen a few times. "Do you have his phone number?"

He rattled off an 800 number.

She dutifully filled it in, then turned the clipboard around for him to sign the bottom of the form. His scribble was firm, slanted and barely legible.

She flipped the form over and started on the profile on the back. "Height? Six-four, six-five?" she guessed.

"Five. Two-forty."

And not an ounce of fat to spare, she knew from experience. She wrote down his weight.

"No drug allergies." She glanced at him. "Right?" She remembered it from his medical chart from Connecticut.

"Right."

She quickly dashed down the items. "Previous surgeries?"

He gave her a dry look. "It would take more than the back of that sheet of paper to list them all."

"Any history of heart disease? Stroke? Diabetes? On your mother's side or your father's?"

"No idea. They died when I was a kid."

Her fingers tightened around her pen. "I'm sorry."

He shrugged as if it didn't matter.

"Who took care of you?"

One of his eyebrows peaked. "That on the form, too?"

"Obviously not." She studied him. Everything about

him now screamed *capable*. *Loner*. But he hadn't always been. At one time in his life, he'd been young. A child.

A parentless child.

If he'd had relatives who'd taken him in, they were either gone or he didn't consider them close any longer, since he'd provided Coleman Black's name as his emergency contact.

"Hey, Courtney." Richie, the acne-skinned imaging tech came around the corner, and she tamped down a swell of irritation at the interruption. "What's up?"

Getting Mason's cast repaired, and making certain he hadn't done any harm to his arm beneath, was a lot more important than peeling away the plethora of onion-skin layers surrounding Mason Hyde's life. She showed Richie the crack on Mason's dark blue cast. "Wyatt is going to try to flag down Dr. Flannery to take a look."

Richie nodded. "He'll need films?"

"That's what I'm figuring."

"I'll get the mobile unit."

Richie had barely moved out of sight, when Pierce Flannery strode into the room, his long white doctor's coat flapping behind his long legs. "Courtney," he greeted, his brown gaze warm. "It's nice to see you again."

"Doctor." Courtney smiled and gestured toward Mason, whose eyes had narrowed on the young doctor's face. "This is Mason Hyde. I'm providing his home health care and—" she touched Mason's cast "—unfortunately didn't do a good enough job. His cast is cracked."

"Well." Flannery lifted Mason's arm a few inches and studied it from every angle. "Get a film and we'll see if we need to start from scratch or if we can just patch it up." He looked at Mason, taking him in fully. "What ran over you? A train?"

"A Hummer," Mason said. "Felt like a train when I was bouncing off it onto the side of the road, though."

Courtney blinked a little.

Given his injuries, she'd assumed there'd been some sort of collision involved. But she'd also assumed that he'd been inside a vehicle of his own, at least.

Not that he'd been struck down by one.

"You were on foot?"

"Yeah." He didn't look at her, but at the doctor. "How long's this gonna take?"

"Shouldn't be long, even if we have to take off the cast and put on a new one." The doctor's gaze traveled to Courtney over Mason's head. He smiled. "Though I'll freely admit that if it takes a while, it'll be no hardship, considering the company."

He was flirting with her and obviously didn't care who witnessed it. She kept her smile in place, but made certain not to let it look too friendly. She had no interest in encouraging the doctor. "I'll see what's holding up Richie," she said and headed in the direction the tech had taken.

"So. You a friend of our lovely Nurse Clay?" Once Courtney was gone, the doctor's gaze fixed on Mason.

"Not exactly." Mason could read the younger man well enough. Even if he'd said he *was* a friend—and all that could be implied by that sometimes nebulous term—the doctor would still be interested in Courtney.

Who could blame him?

Courtney was an exceptionally beautiful woman with a smile and friendliness that would have garnered attention even if she hadn't been tall, long-legged and this side of voluptuous.

"But I am concerned with her best interests," he added with a warning edge.

"Good for you," the doctor said, and he seemed to be sincere.

When it came to his work, Mason had a knack for sizing up a person's character. He just didn't seem able to get a bead on this guy. Because he wasn't a subject that Mason was investigating? Or because he obviously had his eye on Courtney?

Either way, it irritated the hell out of Mason.

He didn't like things being cloudy.

"The portable unit is out of commission." Courtney's voice preceded her appearance by a half a second. She moved behind his wheelchair, bringing with her that soft scent of hers. "I'll have to take you over to imaging."

Flannery glanced at his watch, then nodded. "Let me know when you have the films. I've got some calls to take care of and a few patients to see." He looked over Mason at Courtney and smiled.

Just for her.

Mason's casted leg twitched with the urge to sweep the guy off his well-shod feet.

His chair began moving. "I'll make sure you're paged," Courtney told the doctor before rolling Mason out of the exam area.

He felt a grin pushing at his lips.

Unfortunately, it was still there when they reached the imaging department, and she gave him a suspicious look. "What are you looking so pleased about?"

"Nothing. I'll just be glad to get out of here again. Why are you resorting to the online things when you've got a perfectly good specimen in the doc back there?"

Her eyebrows shot up. "I beg your pardon?"

"He's interested in you."

For a moment, she looked lost for words. "That doesn't mean I'm interested in him."

"Why not? Is he a closet nerd or something?"

She laughed a little. "I have no idea. Why do you care?" Her eyes narrowed. "How did you end up getting hit by an SUV, anyway?"

"By getting in its way. Is he married?"

"No, he's not married. And *clearly* you got in the way. I figured that out for my own brilliant self. But… how? Was the driver drunk or something?"

"Or something. Doctors are supposed to be good catches, aren't they?"

She huffed. "I'm not playing catch! And that's all you're going to say? *Or something,*" she deadpanned his flat answer.

"That's all."

She hesitated for a moment. "Were you impaired?"

He frowned. "What?" Given everything, maybe he shouldn't have been shocked by the question, but he was.

And then, considering the concern in her amber-colored eyes, it was just impatience that rolled through him. "Hell. *No.*" He shook his head. "Believe me, honey. Until I became *impaired* by these damn injuries, I haven't even been tempted. Not once in a decade."

She studied him. "Actually, I believe you. Maybe it wasn't even an accident at all. Was he aiming for you?"

Mason let out a noisy breath. "You're not going to leave this alone, are you?"

"If you didn't want me to be curious, then you shouldn't have said anything about it at all when Dr. Flannery asked."

The fact that she was right didn't help him any.

He looked around the empty waiting room. "No. He

wasn't aiming for *me*. How long's this X-ray going to take, anyway?"

"As long as it takes," she returned smoothly. Then she made a face. "I don't know." She walked across the waiting area and disappeared through an open doorway, returning a few minutes later. "You'll be up next, after they finish with the patient already back there."

She sat on the edge of a molded plastic chair and plucked the clip out of her hair. She closed her eyes as the long blond strands tumbled around her shoulders and raked her fingers through them before twirling it back up into the fat clip. Then she opened her eyes again.

She looked tired.

"Would you still be sleeping if we weren't here?"

Her fine, level brows pulled together. "It doesn't matter."

It mattered to him. "You don't have to stay. I don't need a babysitter. Go track down Flannery. He'll probably ask you out on a date."

"Considering that you somehow put a crack in your cast, I'm not so sure you *don't* need a babysitter. But I wouldn't go back to sleep, even if I went home, so quit using that as an excuse to get rid of me and my curiosity. And if I wanted a date with Dr. Flannery, I'd get one. So drop it." She pushed to her feet. "I'll be back." She pointed at him. "Don't move."

"Funny girl."

She smiled faintly as she went through the doorway once more.

She was gone a little longer this time.

Long enough for a tired-looking woman to walk in carrying a brown-haired little girl with a heavily bandaged wrist. The woman gave Mason a wary look and took one of the chairs in the far corner of the room.

He'd had similar reactions from strangers before, just not when he was obviously laid up with injuries. He knew he looked like some version of scary hell, particularly as unshaven and unkempt as he was now.

He gave her a nod and a smile, but she didn't look comforted by it, and he stifled a sigh.

Mason wished Courtney would return. Playing verbal games with her was a helluva lot better than just sitting here inside the hospital. Scaring perfectly innocent people with the way he looked wasn't anything he particularly relished.

Fortunately, a girl in a white lab coat appeared and gestured to the woman. They disappeared through the same doorway Courtney had, and Mason waited alone a little longer until the waiting was wearing down his last nerve.

He shifted awkwardly in the chair and tried to ignore the itch on his calf beneath the cast by even more awkwardly trying to wheel the chair through the doorway after her. He'd made it far enough to get wedged between the protrusion of his leg and the angle of the chair, when Courtney reappeared.

She stopped at the sight of him and crossed her arms, tilting her head to one side. "Looks like you're almost stuck between a rock and a hard place."

It was truer than she knew.

Her eyes glinted when he said nothing. "Would you like some help?"

"Would you like to cut the sarcasm?"

"Maybe if you weren't so thickheaded and could possibly, just possibly, do what you are asked—"

"Told, you mean."

"—then I might be able to cut the sarcasm."

"Just move the damn chair, would you?"

She tsked and, reaching around him, pushed the chair back several inches until his cast was no longer jammed in the doorway.

Her head was inches from his. "I'm going to take you back there," she said softly and so sweetly that it made his teeth hurt. "But you're going to have to wait for Richie for about five minutes. He's still with someone else. Think you can be a good boy for that long?"

Maybe it was the ironic glint in her amber eyes.

Maybe it was the proximity of her head to his.

Maybe it was just for the hell of it.

He hooked his left hand around her neck and watched her pupils flare. "I'm no boy," he murmured. "And we both know I can be good."

Then he tugged her forward a few inches and caught her mouth with his.

Chapter Five

Before her common sense took over, Courtney felt herself sinking oh-so-dangerously into his kiss. Her heart bumped unevenly inside her chest, and her hands found his shoulders, her fingers pressing through his T-shirt to the warmth beneath.

"Ahem." The sound vaguely registered. And when it was repeated—who knew how many times—it finally penetrated.

She straightened like a shot.

Her gaze skittered over Mason's face and landed on Wyatt Mead's. The tall, lanky male nurse had a grin visible above his short goatee and a twinkle in his gray eyes.

Her lips tingled, but she stared down her coworker as she slipped behind Mason's chair and somehow managed to wrap her nerveless hands around the handles. "Is Richie ready?"

Wyatt looked even more amused. "Not as ready as you two, but yeah."

Courtney ignored the comment and pushed Mason into the first of the three imaging suites, where Richie was waiting near the X-ray table. Courtney positioned Mason's chair next to him and, when the technician took over arranging Mason's arm where he needed, avoided Mason's gaze as she practically fled from the room.

Wyatt was waiting in the corridor outside, his eyebrows raised. "Well, well, well," he teased. "The elusive and untouchable Ms. Clay does like a touch now and then."

"Shut up, Wyatt." She brushed past him, only to turn and give him a pointed glare, complete with pointed finger. "If this gets around, I'll know exactly who to blame."

"Who, me?" He pressed his hand against his chest and tried to look innocent. "All I was doing was coming back to let you know that Rodney will be here soon." He was the hospital's on-call orthopedic technician. Whether Mason's cast needed to be repaired or replaced, Rodney Stewart would be the one to do it.

"Thank you. But I mean it, Wyatt. Keep your mouth shut, or I'll make certain that you'll never get a date with an available girl in this town again." It wasn't that Wyatt wasn't a perfectly good-looking guy. But he was an R.N. and, sad to say, in Weaver, male nurses were still an oddity. Some of the locals were slow to get past it, which is why Courtney had set the guy up on more than one date with a few of her friends. He was shy until you got to know him, and the reports she'd gotten back were that he was fun and interesting, but so far the right match hadn't been made.

Which was sad, too, because Wyatt was one of those

rare breeds of men who *wanted* a commitment. He wanted a wife and kids and the whole shebang.

Now, he was just tsking at Courtney as if her threat was beneath her.

"I don't gossip," he said.

She snorted. "Everyone in this town gossips," she returned. Next to ranching, it seemed to be the preferred occupation. Even among her own family, the tendency thrived.

She had no desire for people to start wagging their tongues about her kissing anyone, and even less desire for word of that to reach her family. Considering her mother ran the hospital, it could reach *her* ears even quicker than most. "I'm just asking you—in this one instance—to forget what you saw."

"Get me a date with Dee Crowder."

Dee was an elementary school teacher who worked with Courtney's cousin Sarah Scalise. "Are you trying coercion?"

"Is it working?"

"Ask her out yourself, Wyatt. For heaven's sake, you see her every morning over at Ruby's when you're both stopping in for coffee before work."

"She's always flirting with people."

"She'd probably flirt with you, too, if you managed to give her a smile instead of just staring into your coffee and mumbling good morning." From inside the suite, she could hear Richie talking to Mason and knew that he'd be finished soon. "I'll put a bug in Dee's ear, okay? But—" she pointed her finger into Wyatt's face "—not unless you promise."

He smiled and crossed his fingers over his heart.

She exhaled noisily and rolled her eyes heavenward.

"You're a great guy, Wyatt. I wish you'd have a little more confidence in yourself. You're not shy with me."

"Yeah, but you make it easy." He gave her a wink and walked away.

"Seems to me you've got plenty of guys around here interested in you."

She turned and looked at Mason.

Richie was obviously done with him.

"Wyatt is not interested in me." She moved behind Mason to take control of his wheelchair and push him back to the emergency room.

"Every guy who isn't related to you is interested." His voice was dry.

She wasn't interested in "every" guy. Just one. And even if she hadn't already known it herself, he'd made it perfectly plain all those months ago that he wasn't interested in anything permanent.

Just remember what you're doing this for, she reminded herself.

She wasn't taking care of Mason out of any hope that something lasting would develop between them. She was taking care of him so that she'd have something lasting. Period.

A child.

"No comment?" Mason asked. "Because you know I'm right?"

Just to suit herself, she made a face at the back of his head. "No," she assured witheringly. "Because there's no point in responding to such ridiculousness."

"Courtney. I heard you were here this morning."

She nearly jumped out of her skin at her mother's voice and came to a stop with the chair, waiting for her lab-coated mother to reach them. "My patient had a little accident," Courtney greeted.

But her mom was already smiling with warmth into Mason's face as she took his good hand in both of hers. "Mr. Hyde," she greeted. The pale brown eyes that she'd passed on to Courtney were warm and sparkling. "It's been over a year since you've been to town. It's good to see you again. I'd ask how you're doing, but that seems a bit unnecessary under the circumstances."

Feeling strangely on edge, Courtney shifted. She'd almost forgotten that Mason had met her parents, too, when he'd been in Weaver. "Mason accidentally cracked his cast. We're here to get it fixed."

Her mother gave her a mild look. "It happens." She turned back to Mason. "If you're feeling up to it, you must come have dinner with us. I know Sawyer would enjoy seeing you again."

"My social calendar is pretty tight these days, but I'll do what I can."

Rebecca laughed, and her still-dark hair bounced around her shoulders. "You're frustrated with the inactivity." She patted his hand. "I have some experience with men like you." She glanced at Courtney. "Bring him by the house before you go on shift tonight. We'll have dinner, and we'll get him back to your place when he gets tired of us old fogies."

"Dr. Clay," Mason drawled, "if you're considered an old fogy, then getting older suddenly has a lot more appeal."

Rebecca laughed again, then shook her head when her name was paged. "Duty calls. See you both later." She hurried off in the direction she'd come from.

Courtney let out a careful breath. She wasn't necessarily surprised at her mother's hospitality toward Mason.

But she still felt a little awkward about it.

She'd never taken a former one-night stand home to have dinner with the folks.

"We going to just sit here in the corridor?" Mason finally asked. "Or do you want me to do this under my own steam?"

Flushing, she quickly pushed his chair the rest of the way to the emergency room. "I've seen the results of your steam," she reminded. "It ended up with you on the floor at my house and also wedged in a doorway. Your steam needs to chill for a while."

"Your father used to be the sheriff, didn't he?"

His conversational leap threw her.

But then, most everything about Mason threw her.

She turned into the emergency room. One of the curtained areas was now occupied. "He used to be. Now Max Scalise is. He's married to my cousin Sarah."

"Lot of family around here."

"Yup." She grinned. "I could give you a rundown on the family tree, but it would take the rest of the afternoon." She locked his wheels next to an empty exam table and, with a swift yank, pulled the long curtain around the area until they were fully enclosed. "Do you feel like stretching out, or do you want to stay seated?"

"Seated," he said immediately. "I've spent enough time flat on my ass."

"Since you were so mysteriously hit by an SUV," she concluded.

He shrugged.

Realizing she was staring a little too hard at the darkening beard on his face, she grabbed his chart and flipped it open. Then she opened one of the drawers in the stainless steel cabinet and pulled out a digital thermometer similar to the one she had at home, as well as a spare stethoscope.

"What are you doing?" He leaned his head back in avoidance when she fitted a clean sleeve on the thermometer and turned toward him.

"Making use of the time." Before he could make some sort of issue about it, she tucked the thermometer in his ear long enough to get a reading. Then she popped the sleeve in the trash, noted his temp—only a few degrees high and much better than it had been during the night—and set the thermometer back in the drawer before turning toward him with the stethoscope.

But Mason caught her wrist in his hand before she reached him. "Stop."

"I'm just—"

He gave her a hard look. "Courtney, if you put your hands on me again, I'm going to kiss you. Again. Are you ready for that?"

A nervous frisson chased down her spine and her fingers curled into her palm. For a moment long enough to shock her, she was tempted. Sorely tempted.

He was her *patient.*

She wasn't supposed to be more interested in tasting his seductive kiss than she was in maintaining some semblance of professionalism.

With a quick twist, she jerked her wrist free and caught his in hers instead. She had just enough time to enjoy the sight of *his* surprise before his hand was free from hers. "Where'd you learn how to do that?"

"My father was the sheriff," she reminded. She leaned closer and lowered her voice. "And I've been surrounded by people like *you* all of my life. They all made sure I know how to protect myself."

The slide of the curtain had her straightening with a jerk, just in time for Dr. Flannery to appear.

"Fortunately, the X-ray didn't show any fresh damage to the bones," he said without preamble.

"Good. The sooner I get out of here, the better."

"Can't say I blame you," Dr. Flannery told him, though his smile was aimed at Courtney. "Although I think the scenery here is better than it is in most places."

Mason caught Courtney's gaze before she could turn away. She wasn't sure if he looked amused or challenging. Maybe both.

"The crack in the cast is significant, though. Rather than chance its integrity, I'd like it replaced entirely. Once that's done, you are free to go," the doctor told Mason as he scribbled on the medical chart. When he was done, he left it sitting on the steel counter next to the sink. "Feel free to call if you have any questions or concerns. Courtney has my number."

As he watched the doctor walk away, Mason figured he'd chew off his own casts if he had to, before he'd call this guy about anything.

Courtney was crouched in front of the steel cabinet, fussing with something in the bottom of it. The back of her T-shirt rode up the small of her back a few inches, taunting him with the sight of her warm, creamy skin above the slight gape of her pants. His fingertips curled down against the vaguely rough texture of his fiberglass cast.

He knew her skin there was smooth. As smooth as his cast was not.

Dammit.

He'd been in Weaver for less than twenty-four hours and already the memories that he'd worked hard to lock away were back with a vengeance. Filling his head. Filling his gut.

He shoved his fingers through his hair, grimacing. He

hadn't had a decent shower since the accident, though the nurses at the hospital in Connecticut had given him sponge baths and washed his hair a few times.

What he wouldn't give for just five minutes under a steaming-hot spray of water.

His gaze drifted back to the enticing curve of Courtney's hips.

Five minutes under a freezing-cold spray of water would probably do him more good.

"What are you doing down there?"

She glanced at him over her shoulder. The action only succeeded in pulling that shirt a half an inch higher.

He felt sweat breaking out at the base of his spine.

"I'm checking the supplies for your cast. Making sure Rodney has everything he needs." She put her hands on her thighs and pushed to her feet. "The only kits I've got here are hot pink or light pink." She smiled a little wickedly. "Interested in either one?"

"I don't have anything against pink," he murmured. "You were wearing pink that night. Liked it real fine, then."

Her cheeks went rosy. Proof positive that she knew exactly what "that" night was. "I told you to forget about that."

"Pink scrubs." Knowing he was tormenting himself wasn't enough to stop him from needling her. "Pink bra. And matching pink panties with that thin, little ribbon stretching over your hips." He'd taken great pleasure in untying that particular ribbon. Taking his sweet time while she'd breathed his name and pleaded for him to go faster....

Her lips parted. "Mason." Her voice was low. Hoarse. "You're not making this any easier."

Like a switch being thrown, regret replaced desire.

He'd pushed at her because he was a slug. Because he knew he wanted her, still, and his ego didn't like feeling alone.

So now his ego was fed.

She wanted him, too.

It was plain on her face. In the drowsy, melting caramel of her eyes and the soft, parted pout of her full lips.

Which got them exactly where?

Nothing had changed since that Valentine's Day.

She was still who she was.

More importantly, he was still who he was.

A former drug addict with a face that scared most people and a career no woman should get remotely near.

He cleared his throat. "I don't care what color the cast is."

Something in her eyes flickered. She hesitated for a moment as if she wanted to say something. But then she nodded. "I know somewhere we have the same blue as what you've already got. I'll go find it." She stepped beyond the curtain enclosing the exam area.

From somewhere nearby, a baby started wailing.

Mason pinched his eyes closed. Just then, he figured things would've been better if he'd stayed at the hospital in Connecticut. Maybe he'd have been able to handle it. Maybe he wouldn't.

But at least there, he wouldn't have been continually confronted by the one woman even his good sense couldn't seem to resist.

It took another few hours, but finally—possessing a new cast that looked identical to the one that had been cut off—Axel dropped off Mason and Courtney again at her place.

It was nearly noon.

"I'll get you some lunch," she said once they were inside.

"You don't have to wait on me."

She raised her brows and gave him a look. "That's one of the things you're paying me for, remember?" She didn't wait for an answer but headed into the kitchen. A moment later, he heard the back door, and then Plato was trotting into the house, coming straight for him.

The dog sniffed at Mason's casts, then turned tail and trotted back into the kitchen to his mistress.

Factually, what Courtney had said about payment was accurate. Truthfully, however, it made him feel like some sort of weak weasel, even though he logically knew that in his present condition, he was more of a hindrance than any sort of help.

He was sitting on the couch, and his crutches, including the one he'd fallen over trying to reach, were still lying next to it. He grabbed them and, with steady determination, managed to get himself on his feet without crashing over again.

Her telephone was still sitting on the dining room table. Next to it were his pain pills.

He eyed them for a long moment. Then he snatched up the bottle and carried it down the hall and into the bathroom.

He managed to pry the lid off and poured the pills out into the palm of his right hand. The little round pills looked even whiter next to the dark blue of his cast.

He exhaled and let them fall into the toilet. Then he flushed and watched them swirl away for good.

Inside, he felt a little lighter.

Which left him with only one remaining dangerous temptation. One he could do nothing about.

Courtney.

The other temptation facing him was the shower, and he eyed the tub with admitted want. He shouldn't have Courtney, but he would have that. He couldn't get his cast wet, and getting in and out would be a challenge with one leg immobilized, but desperate times made for creativity. Sooner or later, he would have to figure it out, or he'd be enlisting Courtney to hose him off in the backyard like she was giving a bath to Plato.

Then he looked in the mirror. His reflection was enough to make him wince. And he was used to the sight.

He fumbled with his shaving kit, managing to get it unzipped. He was right-handed, so shaving with his left didn't come easy, but he did it anyway since he didn't want to chance getting the fresh cast wet. Last thing he needed was another half day spent whiling away the hours at the hospital—where every male above drinking age seemed to be infatuated with Courtney—because he'd done something else damaging to the cast.

Once his jaw was more or less shaved—save a few nicks—he tossed enough water over his head to shove his hair back and out of his face. Then he brushed his teeth and, feeling somewhat more human, hobbled back out to the living area.

He could hear her still moving around in the kitchen. He raised his voice. "Mind if I use your computer?"

"Help yourself."

Balancing on the crutch and his good leg, he hooked the desk chair and pulled it out enough to sit sideways. His leg cast bumped the desk, and a dull throb took up residence in his knee.

He ignored it and covered the computer mouse with his right hand. His arm was immobilized from his biceps to his wrist, but his fingers were free and working perfectly well. He clicked the button, and the swirling screen saver on her computer monitor disappeared.

The website she'd been looking at the night before came into view.

His lips tightened. With one click he could have closed the website. But he hesitated.

Hair color? Any.

Eye color? Any.

He frowned at the next search option. Blood type?

"Oh, wait." Courtney's rushed voice came from behind him. "I forgot something. Let me just—"

He glanced back at her. She was holding a butter knife in one hand and a piece of bread in the other. "*Specimen* type? What the hell kind of matchmaking site is this?"

Her lips pressed together for a moment. "It's not that kind of website," she finally said. Then she sighed noisily, her hands gesturing with the knife and slice of bread. "You can see for yourself what it is."

He looked back at the glowing computer screen. "Yeah. I can see." Some place called Big Sky Cryobank. "Question is, why are you looking at sperm donors?"

Despite the rise of color in her cheeks, her chin lifted slightly. "For heaven's sake, Mason. Why do you think?"

He didn't like the suspicion curling through him. It was the kind of suspicion that made a person feel nervous. Sick. "Someone wants a baby."

"Not someone. *Me.*" She moistened her lips. Her gaze was steady. Almost defiant. "*I* want to have a baby."

Confirmation didn't make his gut settle down any. *"Why?"*

She huffed. "Why not?"

His brain felt like it had been scrambled. "You're young! You've got plenty of time to find a husband." He had to force out the words now even though he'd spent the past year and a half reminding himself of that very fact. "And *then* have a family."

She started to fold her arms over her chest, then seemed to remember the bread and knife she was holding and stopped. "You're sounding very old-fashioned. I don't want a husband," she said distinctly. "I want a baby."

He hadn't thought he was particularly old-fashioned, but maybe he was when it came to some things.

Or some people.

"Borrow someone else's baby for an afternoon," he suggested rapidly. "God knows that family you're in seems to pop 'em out regularly."

She looked heavenward and shook her head. "I'm not going to debate this with you." She went back into the kitchen. "Do you want mustard on your ham sandwich?" she called out a moment later.

He didn't give a flip about mustard or the lack of it.

He looked back at the computer screen and scrolled up to the top of the webpage, then to the bottom.

Her criteria for the donor were broad.

She didn't seem to care about ethnic origins or ancestry or religious backgrounds. She didn't care about physical characteristics. The only thing she had selected was that the donor have *some* college.

Some.

Not even a degree.

The father could be any mug off the street who needed to make a few bucks by donating his genetic cocktail to a sperm bank.

He grimaced.

There was nothing about the situation that he liked. Nothing.

"What does your family think about all this?"

He heard the clink of a dish. Then she came into the living room and set a plate containing an enormous sandwich next to him on the desk. "They don't know yet. I'll get your antibiotics. You can take it after you eat that."

Impatience with his casts rolled through him when she turned and walked away and he wasn't able to stop her. "Why haven't you told them?"

She didn't answer until she returned with his antibiotics in one hand and a bottle of water in the other. "Because there was no reason to, yet. Do you need Tylenol?"

"What do you plan to do? Wait until they can see you're pregnant for themselves?"

"No," she said witheringly. "I saw no point in telling them until I had the means to even do it. I know my family. They know me. They'll be supportive, just like they always are. Not that this is any of your business, anyway." She set the pills and the water next to the plate and pulled the Tylenol bottle out of her pocket and tossed it on his lap. "Eat the sandwich and take the pills." She turned on her heel again, only to stop. She pointed at the table. "What'd you do with the pain pills that were sitting there?"

"Afraid I'm taking them?"

She gave him a steady look. "Are you?"

"I flushed them," he said flatly. "And no. I don't plan to get more."

She probably had no idea the way her eyes could soften.

But he did.

"Good for you." Then she blinked and was all back-to-business. "I still need a shower before I take you to visit my parents. If you want to change clothes before we go, let me know."

He exhaled, watching her walk away. Again.

Impatience rolled through him. Just because she clearly considered this baby business a closed subject didn't mean he did. When he heard the slam of her bedroom door, he turned back to the computer.

He didn't live under a rock.

He knew there were lots of reasons—some very good reasons—why individuals chose the services of a sperm donor.

But Courtney?

It just didn't go with his vision of her and the wholly perfect life she was supposed to have someday.

With someone else.

Someone deserving. Someone good enough for her.

He shoved half the sandwich in his mouth, even though it tasted like sawdust, and choked it down with water. He swallowed the pills.

He could hear the faint sound of water running.

He shook his head and grabbed the crutches. His back twanged warningly when he moved too fast, but he didn't slow.

He reached her bedroom and knocked. When she didn't answer, he pushed open the door.

Plato was lying on the floor next to her bed, and he lifted his head, giving Mason a steady glare.

Mason ignored him. The door to her en suite bathroom was ajar, steam rolling out near the floor, and he walked past the dog to it. "What do you mean, *means?*" he said loudly through the opening.

He heard her squeak of alarm, followed immediately by a low sound from the dog behind him. "Don't you dare come in here!"

He hadn't been planning on it, but Courtney's warning sure did make him want to. He pressed his forehead against the white-painted door frame and reminded himself that he wasn't a complete bastard. "What means?" he asked again.

The rush of water cut off. He heard the rattle of a shower curtain being drawn, and for half a second, his brain took a short circuit along the path of her nude, wet body.

Then the door was yanked open, and she stood there, covered from neck to red-painted toes in a thick pink robe. Her hair was a tangled mass streaming down her back. Her face was shiny clean, her amber eyes sparkling between water-spiked eyelashes. Heat streaked through him.

"Financial means," she said crisply. "Thanks to *you,* I can now afford to get pregnant. And sooner rather than later!"

Then she shut the door right in his face, the click of the door lock sounding loud and final.

Chapter Six

Courtney's Friday night shift, Mason learned later that day, ran from 7:00 p.m. to 7:00 a.m.

Practically the only words she'd exchanged with him, once she'd finally come out of her bedroom, were whether or not he wanted to get out of the invitation her mother had extended.

The fact that she'd obviously hoped he did want to get out of it was the only reason he'd said he didn't.

And they said that women were the contrary creatures.

Which was why he found himself awkwardly positioned in the backseat of her little car after enduring the humbling activity of having to enlist her aid just to put on a cut-up pair of jeans.

She hadn't seemed the least bit fazed by any of it. Thank God he'd been able to manage the shirt on his own.

"How soon?" he asked to the back of her head as she drove through town.

"Until we get to my parents' house? Not long."

"How soon until you plan to knock yourself up?"

"Lovely phrase," she said drily.

"Isn't it accurate?"

He saw her shoulders shrug. "I have to see an OB first. My sister-in-law, Mallory, is one, so I'll see if she's willing to sign off on my paperwork with the cryobank and perform the procedure. Hopefully, I'll be pregnant by the end of the year."

He could see the smile on her face through the rear-view mirror. "I can see the future now. Little Johnny or Mary comes to Mommy and asks where they come from. And she says…from a *procedure*."

"I cannot believe you're so bothered by this."

"I'm not bothered," he denied. "Just…playing devil's advocate. You've figured out how to get pregnant without a man around. But what about after that? Raising a child is an expensive proposition. It isn't just the cost of having a baby. Or in your case, buying some guy's—"

"I get it," she cut him off. "And I'm well aware of the cost. From conception to college." Her gaze met his in the rearview mirror. "Fortunately, this little gig with you while you recuperate is going to get me at least through the conception part. It's not exactly covered by my health insurance."

He grimaced. Her words didn't sit well. Not when every cell he possessed—even the ones still broken and bruised—tripped over themselves wanting to do a little baby-making the old-fashioned way. With no baby as the end result, of course.

He nearly got a rash just thinking about it.

"Okay. So forget the cost. Bringing up a baby on your own isn't going to be an easy task."

"I have a very involved, very loving family," she returned, her voice beyond patient. "I'm never alone."

"You know what I mean. Statistics show that two parents are better than one."

"I'm not interested in your statistics, Mason." Her voice turned cool. "Please drop it. And please keep your thoughts to yourself about this when we get to my parents'. I hardly want to break the news to them while you're there, glowering."

"Thought you said they would jump for joy at the news. And I'm not glowering."

She snorted. "What I said was that they'd be supportive when the time comes. And you most certainly *have* been glowering. Ever since you saw the website on my computer. I get it, all right? You don't approve."

"I think there are better ways."

She pulled up to a stoplight, one of the few that the small town possessed.

She looked over her seat at him. "Like what? Getting pregnant by a man I have no intention of becoming involved with?"

"Isn't that what you're planning to do with one of those spermsicles?"

She rolled her eyes and turned back to the road in front of her. "That's a horrible term."

"Stuff comes frozen, doesn't it?"

The light turned green, and she started through the intersection with a jerk. "What did you do? Read the frequently asked questions section on the website? Or do you just happen to have a lot of knowledge about the subject?"

He had read the FAQ section…mostly with a fair amount of morbid interest.

"You're young and beautiful. You should have the

world by the tail. Why the hell do you want to order this stuff off the internet?"

She turned off the main road onto a narrower, curving one. "Because it's convenient." Her voice was crisp. "There doesn't happen to be a sperm bank in Weaver, in case you hadn't noticed, and I can't exactly be running off to Montana every week to browse through their catalog until I decide who I want to father my baby!" Her voice had risen.

"How do you know it's even legit?"

She made a groaning sound and pulled up in front of a sprawling house surrounded by enough pine trees to populate a Christmas tree lot. "Grant me some credit, would you please? I'm not a fool. I've done my homework. The cryobank I've chosen is very well regarded. It's not like they allow people to put orders in like you would for a book! You have to be under a doctor's care, remember?" She shoved the car into Park so abruptly that he rocked against the seat in front of him. She looked back at him. "Sorry. Now, can we drop the subject before we go inside?"

She didn't wait for an answer but pushed open her car door and got out. Then she opened the passenger door, pulled out his crutches, which were lying across the floor, and gestured. "Come on. Give me your hand."

He looked across at her. "When're you going to order up your frozen future?"

Her lips pressed together, but then she shook her head and let out a laugh. "Oh, my God. Would you please *stop?*"

He realized he had a faint smile on his face, too.

Dammit.

He stretched his good arm toward her, and her palm slid against his until her long fingers wrapped securely around his forearm. Her other hand went beneath his leg cast to help guide it. Using his good leg for leverage, they managed to slide him far enough along the seat so that he could plant his shoe on the ground and finish extricating himself from the car.

She handed him the crutches and then helped him stand.

Whether he liked it or not, she was good at what she did. She gave as much assistance as he needed, until he could power himself under his own steam, and managed not to hover.

Too bad every time she touched him, his nerves danced a damn annoying jig.

"We'll head around to the side door." She gestured toward the house, which was fronted by a walkway formed of several sets of shallow brick steps. "No stairs." She didn't ask him if he needed help, which he appreciated, as she began walking off toward one side of the house.

He planted the crutches and slowly followed. Knowing that he was watching her hind view didn't get him to stop, even when the bottom of his cast caught on an uneven piece of brick.

He'd already landed on his face because of his clumsiness. At least if he landed on his face this time, it'd be because he was admiring a human work of art.

She reached the side door and turned to wait. "Sure can tell it's going to be October in a few days," she said conversationally. "It's getting downright chilly."

He schooled his gaze on her face.

She raised an eyebrow as if she knew perfectly well where his thoughts were.

She probably did. Women who looked like her grew up with men's stares. In that regard, he was no better than anyone else. Maybe he was worse, because he knew exactly what he was doing.

"I suppose I should warn you," she said, "that it's not just going to be my folks here." She jerked her chin. "That's my grandfather's truck parked back there. And if I'm not mistaken, those are a few of my uncles driving up right now, too."

He followed her gaze. A big black pickup was turning toward the house. Almost on its heels was a low-slung sports car.

When he looked back at Courtney, she gave him an almost pitying smile. "Don't worry. They're all harmless. Mostly."

In the course of his work with Coleman Black, Mason had had plenty of opportunity to become acquainted with several members of Courtney's extended family. Some of them had their own history with Cole. Some didn't.

Harmless wasn't one of the words he would have used for any of them.

He exhaled and crutched the rest of the way. "Let's get on with it, then."

She pulled open the wooden screen door and stepped out of his way. The second he went inside the house, they seemed surrounded by people.

Not just Courtney's parents, Sawyer and Rebecca. And her grandparents, Squire and Gloria, and her aunts and uncles. But also cousins. And cousins' spouses.

And children.

He'd seen the Clay family en masse before, so it wasn't seeing them now that seemed a particular shock. But that first time—save the notable night he'd spent in Courtney's bed—he'd been in Weaver on an assignment to help protect Axel's now wife. He'd seen the family through the eyes of a Hollins-Winword agent. He didn't have that particular benefit this time around.

He wasn't sure why it made a difference, but it did.

Now, being around all of these people—these *family* members—made him itchy. On edge.

As if they were all looking at him, wondering what the hell kind of business he had staying under their precious Courtney's roof.

"Here." The woman in question appeared next to where he was sitting—feeling like the elephant in the room—in the center of an oversized leather couch, with his cast propped on an ottoman. She was holding a plate loaded with an immense helping of steaming lasagna and crispy garlic bread. She also was holding a plate with salad on it. "Mom doesn't believe in small helpings, so I hope you're hungry. Which one do you want to start off with?"

"I'm not exactly working off a lot of food these days," he said wryly, as he took the lasagna.

There were so many people there that nobody attempted to crowd around the long table in the window-lined dining room, but instead used every other available seat, including the floor.

"It's no fun being laid up." A petite, slender blonde sank gracefully to the floor next to the couch, her legs folded beneath her. "Even less fun feeling like you've lost your independence as a result. I'm Lucy Buchanan. Courtney's coz." She smiled at him, her aquamarine eyes twinkling. "I'd shake your hand, but mine are presently full of food."

It was an excuse, he knew, because his was stuck in a cast, making a handshake awkward. "You're new," he told her. He was good with people's faces and their names. She hadn't been in Weaver when he'd been there before.

Courtney laughed. She'd kicked off her rubbery clogs that she wore at the hospital, and sat cross-legged on the couch beside him. Her shoulder brushed against his, but she didn't seem to notice as she tucked her fork into the salad. "Luce just moved back home from New York," she told him. "She got engaged a few weeks ago. Speaking of…where are Beck and Shelby?"

"I'm here." A lanky man about Mason's age, bearing a plate as loaded as Mason's, sauntered into the room. "Shelby's spending the night at her friend's." He didn't have the quick tact of his fiancée and stuck out his hand to Mason. He made a wry face when Mason lifted his hand, cast and all. "Ah. Casts suck." Instead of shaking what was visible of his fingers, Beck bumped his knuckles against Mason's. "Beck Ventura."

"Mason Hyde. And yeah. They do," he agreed. "Who's Shelby?"

"Beck's daughter," Courtney said. "She's six."

Mason could practically see the gleam in Courtney's eyes. He figured she was imagining her own future six-year-old daughter.

Rebecca walked into the room. "As you can see, Mr. Hyde, our get-together got a little out of hand." She was wearing jeans and a sweatshirt and was holding a baby on her hip, looking as different as she could get from the white-coated doctor he'd met earlier that day. "That tends to happen around the Clays." She tucked her dark hair behind her ear and grinned.

Courtney had her eyes, he realized. And her grin. "Make it Mason, please."

At the sight of her mother and the baby, Courtney

promptly set aside her partially eaten salad and held out her hands. "Gimme."

Rebecca surrendered the tot, who was wearing a green-footed thing, giving Mason no clue whether it was a boy or a girl. Courtney snuggled the baby close, kissing the child's round little cheek.

"This," she told him, after she came up for air, "is Aidan."

Mason gave the baby a closer look. "Axel's kid?"

"Mmm-hmm." She looked up at her mother. "How'd you get drawn for babysitting duty?"

"She didn't." Another woman wandered into the room. She, too, had long brown hair and was holding a plate of food. Mason recognized her as Axel's mother, Emily. "Aidan's spending the night with Jefferson and me."

She turned her pansy-brown gaze on Mason and smiled. "But we heard *you* were coming for dinner and crashed." She leaned over and brushed her cheek against Mason's. "So good to see you again. I wish it were under better circumstances for you." As if they were old friends, instead of bare acquaintances through his association with her son, she sat next to him on the arm of the couch. "You're letting that lasagna get cold, darling, and you can't heal if you don't eat. Eat."

"Just easier to listen to her," a tall man drawled in a quiet voice as he pulled a chair from the dining room table closer. "That's what I've learned after all these years."

"Jefferson," Mason greeted. The older man was a legend in the murky world of Hollins-Winword, even though he'd gotten out of the business decades earlier. "How's the horse-breeding business?"

"Not as interesting as the cow business," answered a

steel-haired man as he stomped into the room with his cane. "Try telling my son that, though." He gave Jefferson an annoyed look even as he grabbed a chair and planted himself next to him.

Well aware that her grandfather's ornery tones hid a heart as wide as Wyoming, Courtney grinned. "My grandfather," she told Mason. "Squire Clay, this is Mason Hyde. He's the patient renting my spare bedroom."

Squire lifted a hand. "I remember, missy. Not senile yet. We met when Axel was chasing after Tara…and thinking we didn't know what was up." He fixed his sharp, blue gaze on Mason. "He was staying under her roof and getting up to mischief. You gonna do that with my granddaughter?"

"Squire!" Courtney nearly choked.

"Stay out of this, girl." Her grandfather didn't even spare her a look.

"Sir, if you'll pardon my saying so, I'm lucky if I can get up to take a leak," Mason drawled. "Mischief's pretty much out of my immediate future."

Squire let out a bark of laughter and tapped the end of his cane on the floor. "Always like a man who speaks the truth. So. Hear you managed to save that little girl in the process of getting all broke up."

Courtney jerked. She looked at Mason. The vaguely good-natured smile on his face had disappeared. "Little girl? What little girl?"

"McDonohue. McDouglas." Emily shook her head. "Name's something like that, anyway. I saw an article on the internet about it a few days ago."

"Pushed the little filly right out of the way of a truck," Squire interjected. "Saved her life, so they say. Seems to me, it's a wonder you didn't end up getting killed."

Absently jiggling Aidan on her lap, Courtney watched Mason. He was jabbing at his lasagna and clearly didn't want to pursue the subject. "Who was she? Did you know her?"

"Just a kid who didn't have the sense not to walk in the street." He shoved the last bite of lasagna in his mouth and pushed the plate at her. "Mind if I have more?"

Perfectly aware that he'd pretty much dodged her question, she took the plate and rose, taking the baby— who'd tightly twined his little fists in her loose hair— with her. Mason could be as closemouthed as he wanted. She would just hunt around on the internet and find the article her aunt had referred to, and she would know the story, soon enough.

Even if a part of her did wish that he'd tell her himself.

In the kitchen, she handed Aidan off to her mother, who was talking with a few more of Courtney's aunts, worked her hair free and added another helping from one of the multiple pans on the counter.

"So." Her aunt Jaimie tilted her auburn head and stepped right in Courtney's way before she could go back to the living room. "What's this I hear about you kissing your patient at the hospital today?"

Courtney's jaw loosened. "What?" She shot her mother a look. Rebecca just seemed amused as Aidan batted his palms against her hand. "I don't know what you're talking about," she lied.

The first chance she got, she was going to skin Wyatt Mead.

"Lip-locking," Jaimie enunciated, laughter crinkling the skin around her vivid green eyes. "With Mr. Hyde.

And I'm pretty sure that's a term that translates even to you young people."

"I can't imagine where you get your information," Courtney insisted. "You know what gossip is like in this town."

Maggie, yet another one of Courtney's aunts, laughed outright. "Sadly, that gossip is almost always founded on some kernel of truth."

"Where there's smoke, and all that," Jaimie agreed.

Courtney's cheeks felt like they were on fire, and there was no chance whatsoever that the women surrounding her couldn't see the flush. Or correctly interpret its cause. "I'm going to kill Wyatt," she muttered through her teeth.

Rebecca smiled faintly. "Fortunately, you weren't on duty, so it's not as if you were breaking any sort of hospital rule that I'd have to write up."

"Of course, if your grandfather hears about it," Courtney's grandmother, Gloria, warned humorously, "who knows what will happen. You know how protective he is of all his girls."

Emily had wandered into the crowded kitchen, and she rolled her eyes. "Fortunately, Squire has mellowed a little over the years since he kicked Jefferson out of his own home for having his eye on me when *I* was young." Perfectly at home in her sister-in-law's house, she found a mug and poured coffee into it.

"Grandchildren and great-grandchildren—" Jaimie tickled Aidan under the chin "—have mellowed Squire." She wryly corrected Emily. "The years that have passed have been purely incidental."

Whether Squire had mellowed any or not was moot as far as Courtney was concerned. She didn't want people gossiping about her. Not even her own family, whether it was good-natured or not. "I'm taking this plate back in to Mason and I don't want to hear another word about—" she waved her hand at the older women "—any of that." As she left the kitchen, she caught the surprised looks on their faces in the half breath before they all broke into laughter.

Her molars ground together. Wyatt was dead meat.

She hurried over to Mason and handed him his plate, even as she nudged her feet into her shoes. "I need to get to the hospital." She looked around the room, her gaze finally landing on her father. He was standing near the windows that overlooked the rear of their property, talking to Daniel and Matthew, who were married to Maggie and Jaimie. "You'll get Mason—" she barely prevented herself from saying *home* "—back to my place later?"

Her dad nodded.

She hadn't really doubted that he'd agree, but she was more than a little nervous about what kind of conversations might ensue in her absence.

Fortunately, Mason was looking as if he weren't in the mood to talk, and she was hoping that meant he wouldn't decide to take the initiative and start talking *spermsicles* with her family.

She stopped next to him, pulled his bottle of antibiotics out of her pocket and handed them to him. "Don't forget."

"Yes, ma'am." His voice was arid.

"I'll see you in the morning, then. Try not to break anything else before then."

His lips twisted in a sort of smile. His scar was standing out more than usual, and she suspected he was wishing that he was anywhere else other than here.

Refusing to feel sorry for him, since she'd done her best to talk him out of going to her folks' in the first place, she went over to her grandfather and kissed his cheek. "Behave," she whispered in his ear.

He grunted. "Where's the fun in that?"

She gave him a pointed look. "That's what I'm afraid of."

Then, because she really did need to leave or chance being late for her shift, she quickly gave a general goodbye and hurried out to her car.

Her mother was leaning against the hood.

Courtney swallowed a jolt of nervousness and picked up her pace again until she reached the car. "Did I forget something?"

"How well do you know Mason?"

Courtney hesitated. She wasn't sure what she'd expected, but it wasn't that. "Not well. We met, you know, in passing. When he was here a few years ago working with Axel to protect Tara. Well, it wasn't quite that long ago, but—"

"You're rambling, honey."

Courtney's lips slammed shut. She swallowed again. "I know Axel trusts him, or he wouldn't have suggested any of this," she finally said. "He's a job. Mason doesn't want to be dependent on me for any longer than necessary. His arm should be out of the cast in a month or so. And hopefully, his leg not too long after that. He'll be gone the second he can go."

"Mmm." Her mother pushed away from the car. "Just…be careful, all right?"

That was easy. "I'm always careful," Courtney reminded. "Remember?"

"I do." Her mom followed her around to the driver's side and held the door while Courtney climbed behind the wheel. "I was careful, too, when I first met your father."

Courtney raised her eyebrows. "Not exactly a cautionary comment, Mom. You and Dad have been married for a long time now." Close to thirty years, in fact.

"But it took us a long time to get to that point," she reminded gently. "Your dad and I did a lot of things wrong—spent a lot of years on it, in fact—before we managed to get it right. I'm just saying…be careful."

"I know exactly what I want out of life," Courtney assured her with more blitheness than she felt. "Mason is not going to get in the way of my plans."

Unfortunately, as her mother shut the door and moved back from the car, she didn't look quite convinced. "Drive carefully," was all she said.

Courtney couldn't help but grin at that, considering the hospital was less than five miles away. "Thanks for entertaining him," she said, before she drove off.

The first thing she did when she got to the hospital was corner Wyatt, who was just getting off his shift. "Guess you don't want that date with Dee Crowder that badly," she told him.

He gave her a surprised look. "What are you talking about?"

"About *you* talking!"

"I didn't." He defended himself. "I didn't say a word to anyone!"

"Not *any*one?"

"Well, Greer. But she wouldn't say anything."

Courtney groaned. "That's exactly how things get out. We trust someone not to say anything to anyone, and then they do, and they trust that person not to say anything, and then *they* do." She threw up her hands and walked to the nurse's lounge to store her purse in her locker. "I'll be lucky if this town doesn't have us married and pregnant by morning," she muttered.

"Who's pregnant?" Carrying an enormous cup of coffee, Lisa Pope walked into the lounge.

"Nobody."

Her coworker's gaze turned crafty. "Any practicing to *get* that way going on?"

Courtney groaned and walked out of the lounge.

It was going to be a long shift.

Chapter Seven

She was over an hour late getting off shift the next morning, but when she quietly let herself into her house, Courtney was still surprised to see Mason up.

He was sitting at her computer desk, and at first she feared he was poking around on the cryobank site again. He wouldn't find it difficult to locate since she had all of her favorite sites clearly saved.

"You're up early," she greeted as she walked across the living room, kicking off her shoes as she went. When she was closer, her nerves relaxed a little.

He was on some network news site.

"And you're off work late," he returned. He gave her a narrow-eyed look. "You look like hell."

"Well—" she smiled tiredly "—don't feel like you need to sugarcoat it or anything."

He swiveled—more or less, considering his cumbersome casts—to face her. "What happened?"

She shook her head as she walked past him into the kitchen. "Just a long night. What's your stand on eggs and toast?" She glanced outside the back door and saw Plato sleeping contentedly in a sunbeam. "You let the dog out. Thanks."

"No prob. And you don't have to cook for me."

"Part of the deal," she reminded. Her eyes felt glazed as she turned her attention to the maple cupboards in front of her. "But it's Saturday morning. How about pancakes?"

She heard the scrape-thump of his crutches and cast and knew he was coming into the kitchen. She realized she was just standing there, staring at nothing, and quickly opened the cupboard door to pull out a loaf of bread. "Or maybe French toast."

His hand closed over her shoulder, and she jumped an inch. He tugged the bread out of her lax fingers and set it on the counter. "Maybe some sleep."

"I told you, I need to decompress a little after a shift." She picked up the bread again. "And you need to eat."

"I already did." He took the bread and reached past her head to slide it on top of the refrigerator. "I had leftover lasagna that your mother sent back with me last night."

Courtney looked around the kitchen. There wasn't a sign that he'd been in here at all.

"What'd you do? Eat it cold?" She grabbed his day-old cast and ran her fingers along the bottom edge. It was dry. If he'd washed the dishes he'd used, he hadn't gotten the cast wet.

He deliberately moved his arm away. "Yes. And off the paper plate that it was sitting on. And before you ask, I took the damn antibiotics. *Go* get some sleep before you fall over."

Somehow, she found herself being turned out of the kitchen, which was a trick since she was much more agile than he was in his present condition. "I looked you up on the internet," she said, thinking that would stop him.

It didn't. "Figured you would."

"Why? Because you think I'm nosy?" Better that he think that than believe she was insatiably curious where he was concerned.

"I'd go for…inquisitive."

"That's another word for nosy." They passed the dining room table and the computer. The screen was a swirling dervish of colors now. "You didn't say that the girl you saved was Donovan McDougal's daughter. He's famous, for heaven's sake." The European businessman who seemed to dabble in everything from real estate to entertainment was often in the news.

"He's also got a big mouth." Mason's voice was low behind her. Intimate.

Despite herself, her footsteps hesitated. She had to physically draw a breath and ride herd on her imagination.

Intimate?

Hardly. The guy was practically frog-marching her down the hallway.

Mason's chest was a warm wall behind her. His crutches were on either side of her, and the cast on his leg was nudging against her backside. He was wearing the same jeans he'd been wearing the night before. She wondered if he'd slept in them, because she seriously doubted that he'd have been able to pull them back on, even though he could get them off.

She planted her bare feet as much as they could be planted on the wood floor. "Well, according to what the big mouth said, that accident was not an accident at all. You were in Barcelona protecting him because someone was threatening his life. But instead, the person went after his daughter. You were the only one who realized what was happening before it was too late." According to the reports she'd read, Mason had knowingly risked his life for the little girl, tossing her to safety before the vehicle had struck him and plowed uncontrollably into a ravine. Mason had survived with a host of injuries. The deadly driver had not.

"Since you seem to have all the details now, there's nothing else to be inquisitive about. So it's my turn. How do you plan to take care of a baby when you work a night shift like this? Or are you going to be one of those parents who stick their kid in day care all day?"

"There's nothing wrong with proper day care," she said irritably. "And I'll switch to a day shift when the time comes."

"You can just decide to do that? Doesn't a shift have to be available first, or do you figure that you can have your mom arrange things to suit you?"

She slapped her hands out, catching the door frame of her bedroom to halt their momentum, then spun around to look at him.

Her nose was practically buried in the T-shirt covering his chest. The shirt that yesterday he'd insisted he could put on with no assistance.

She carefully stepped back a few inches, pulling her eyes away from the dark swirl of chest hair that was visible in the stretched out V-neck. Her fingertips were suddenly tingling as if they remembered the soft-crisp feel of it, and she pressed them together. "First of all, my mom would never play favorites like that. And you obviously don't know me at all if you think I would even ask! Fortunately for me, there are plenty of nursing jobs in the area. If I can't find a schedule that is more suitable at the hospital, then I'll find one somewhere else." Her spurt of energy dissipated, and she turned away from him again. "Maybe I'll become a school nurse, where the biggest emergencies I'll have to deal with are bloody noses and the occasional case of head lice." At least it wouldn't be likely that she'd have the kind of case they'd had at the hospital that morning.

She pulled off the top of her scrubs, leaving behind the long-sleeved T-shirt she wore underneath.

Somehow, the giant on crutches managed to beat her to the bed. He pulled back her quilt with one tug.

"You're not supposed to do that," she grumbled.

He silently raised an eyebrow.

"Move faster than me."

The corner of his lips curved. "Honey, you're not moving real fast," he pointed out. "Did you become a nurse so you could deal with bloody noses and the occasional bug?"

Now that she was within a foot of her bed, she felt a little like a horse that scented its barn, and she aimed straight for it. "Of course not." Her knee hit the mattress and she went facedown, tugging her pillow against her cheek. "I wanted to help people," she murmured. "My grandmother—Gloria. She was a nurse."

"Yeah. Last night, I heard all about how she and Squire met when she was taking care of him after he had a heart attack."

"Sort of like us." The words drizzled out of her lips without thinking, and as soon as she heard what she'd said, her eyes flew open. "I didn't mean... I was just saying that she was—"

"I know what you were saying." He reached down

and nudged her head onto the pillow. "Close your eyes, Courtney. You're making *me* feel exhausted."

The pillow did feel wonderful. But no less wonderful, she figured, than the sound of her name on his lips.

She closed her eyes, reminding herself that she'd been running on only a few hours of sleep for two days. If she was at the top of her form, she wouldn't be thinking such silly things. "*You're* not supposed to be taking care of *me*," she returned.

"I won't tell anyone."

She felt his hand plucking at the back of her head, and then her ponytail slid free. His fingertips rubbed against her scalp and she couldn't help but sigh. "Mason?"

His rubbing stopped.

She peeled open her heavy lids and looked up at him through her eyelashes. "Do you see a lot of violence working for Hollins-Winword?"

He watched her, unblinking, for a long moment. "Yes."

Her chest went tight. Maybe because he'd given her a straight-out answer. Maybe because she was feeling wrung out from her shift. Maybe because just then, there wasn't a cell in her body that didn't want her to ask him to lie down, casts and all, right beside her. "How do you sleep at night?"

His fingers threaded through her hair once more. "Sometimes I don't."

Now, her throat ached, too. "We had a woman brought in around two this morning. Her husband had been beating her. She had a toddler with her." She felt his sudden stillness.

"What happened?"

"She had massive internal injuries. The husband followed her, evidently intent on finishing the job. It took two deputy sheriffs to contain him."

"Do you know them?"

"No." She rolled onto her back, and his hand fell away from her hair, returning to the grip of his crutch tucked under his arm. "They lived on the other side of Braden. She was trying to get away with the child, but she ran off the road, and the officer on the scene had her brought in. We'd barely gotten her into surgery, when the husband got there."

"And?"

"She didn't survive." She blew out a long breath. "The husband's been charged, and the baby got carted away by social services."

"No other family to take the kid?"

"No. How old were you when you lost your parents?"

"Four."

Her heart ached a little more. "What happened?"

"At the time, the story was a car accident."

"Excuse me?"

"He caught her cheating on him and shot her." His voice was matter-of-fact. "I looked into their deaths when I was an adult."

"Good Lord, Mason." Appalled, she sat up, curling her feet underneath her. "I'm so sorry."

He lifted a shoulder. "I don't remember them."

"You still haven't said who took care of you."

"There's nothing to say. I was in foster care. Too many homes to even remember. Some good. Some not so good. By the time I was fifteen, I was living on my own."

She frowned. "How does a fifteen-year-old boy support himself?"

His lips twisted. "Not very well. But I was a big kid

and I lied well. People believed that I was older. I worked odd jobs when I could."

"And school?"

"That didn't put bread in my mouth. Why are we talking about this? It's old news." He jerked his chin toward the pillows and swung his crutches away from the bedside. "Lie down again. Go to sleep."

"It's not old news to me," she said quietly. "And I'm interested, okay? Maybe I want to know that the little toddler from this morning—who has essentially lost both of his parents—has a chance in life that's better than the doom and gloom of the statistics. You're an honest-to-goodness hero, Mason. You grew up with no parents of your own to become a man who goes out and saves other people's lives. You've battled an addiction and won."

He grimaced. "I'm no hero."

She unwound her legs and climbed off the bed. "Donovan McDougal and his family wouldn't agree. And neither would I."

"You don't know anything about me."

"I know Axel trusts you, or you wouldn't be staying under my roof."

"We've worked together."

"I know you put your life in danger to save someone's child." She gestured at him. "And I'll say it again—or you wouldn't be staying under my roof." Before he could counter with another denial, she stepped closer. "I know you've overcome a lot, not just from your childhood, but as an adult." She touched the scar running down his face. "And I know that, even though you try to hide it, you have a great gentleness in you."

He grabbed her hand and pulled it away from his face. But he didn't let go. "I finished school from jail."

His voice was hard. "After being picked up for breaking and entering. Not so heroic."

He had a firm grip on her hand, but far from punishing.

"Breaking and entering what?"

His brows pulled together. "What the hell difference does it make?"

"I'm just…inquisitive."

"I'm beginning to feel like I'm in the inquisition." He set her hand away from him. "There's nothing admirable about my life. All I've done is survive. I broke into the store one of my former foster parents owned so I could steal the till before it was deposited in the bank. Obviously, I wasn't a very good thief, because I spent a few years behind bars, as a result. I ended up working for Cole soon after, because he's always hunting the dregs of society for…creative souls. I was good at reading people. Good at manipulating situations to my advantage. But not good enough, because the people I was supposed to be protecting nearly ended up dead, and I ended up with this." He waved at his scarred face. "After that, I let myself get hooked on painkillers for too damn long. I lost my wife and I nearly lost my job."

He'd been married? She didn't know why that stunned her, but it did. "What, uh, what did you need the money for?"

"God in heaven, woman! Aren't you listening to anything I'm saying?"

"I'm listening," she returned tartly. "But what I'm trying to do is *understand*."

"I wanted to buy a bus ticket for the foster kid living with that old family of mine so he could get the hell away from them. God knows nobody in charge of the system believed that the churchgoing souls were abusive freaks."

"Oh, Mason."

"Don't get sympathetic. I was a thief. A bad one."

"What happened to the other foster child?"

"How the hell should I know? I was in jail."

"You never tried to find out?"

His lips thinned. "He aged out," he finally said. "Graduated high school and disappeared." He gave her a narrow-eyed stare. "Don't try to understand me anymore. There's no point. Where you're concerned, the only reason I'm here is so you can afford your baby plans. Where I'm concerned, the only reason I'm here is so that Cole doesn't fire my ass."

Her head snapped back. She blinked, almost swaying from the sting. "I, um…right. You're right. This is just a simple business deal." Why couldn't she remember that? She cleared her throat and forced a wry smile that she didn't feel at all. "Blame it on lack of sleep." She snatched up the band that he'd pulled off her ponytail and yanked her hair back once more.

She would *not* think about the feel of his fingers moving through her hair. She would *not* think about a fifteen-year-old boy who'd been desperate enough to break and enter in order to try to help someone else.

She waved her hand toward the door. "Don't close the door all the way. I want to be able to hear if you need something."

He looked at her as if she'd grown a second head. "You're serious."

She was exhausted. She was still saddened about the events at the hospital. And logical or not, she was stinging from his unsubtle reminder that her only purpose for him was born of necessity. Not choice. "Yes." Her voice was flat, and she turned back toward her bed. "That's my job."

Mason bit back an oath. In her place, he'd be telling himself to go to hell. That's what he deserved.

Feeling like the proverbial bull in a china shop, he managed to work his way out of her pretty, unabashedly feminine bedroom without doing any physical damage to her things.

The only damage he'd caused had been emotional.

He turned to look back at her when he reached the doorway.

She was lying on her side, facing away from him. She'd ruthlessly pulled her shining hair into another ponytail, and she'd hooked her arm around a pillow.

"I told you that I'm no hero," he said.

"I believe I was listening when you said it." Her voice was muffled but clear.

He'd wanted to put some distance back between them. Well. He'd succeeded.

He exhaled and pulled the door all the way closed. He'd already been the cause of one day with hardly any sleep for her. He wasn't going to add to it, even if he had to sit on his thumbs for the next eight hours to make sure she had some peace and quiet.

He crutched back to his bedroom. But the books there held no interest for him. As stealthily as he could, he went out to the living area.

He sat at the computer for a while, feeling only a little guilty for browsing all of the sites she'd left open on her screen.

Every single one of them was baby related.

The cryobank site, of course.

But then there was the all-about-baby site that seemed

to have information on everything from the moment after birth to preparing your kid for kindergarten.

And then the home-and-garden site with every decorating and safety tip known to man for making your house baby ready.

She'd even looked at a baby boutique site and added an expensive, engravable silver rattle to something called her "wish list."

He scrubbed his hand down his face and turned off the computer screen.

"Remember what you're doing here, Hyde," he muttered to himself. It wasn't supposed to have anything to do with getting involved in Courtney Clay's life, and it would be better for both of them if he could manage to remember that fact.

He laboriously managed to get onto his feet again and limped his way back to his bedroom.

Before he turned into the room, though, he noticed that Courtney's bedroom door—which he had quietly shut—was ajar.

So she could hear him if he needed her.

He eyed that wedge of open space for a long while.

Then he went into his bedroom and closed the door.

It was the smart thing to do. He knew it.

He still felt like hell.

It was the sound of running water that woke her.

Courtney rolled onto her back and rubbed her eyes. The clock on her nightstand told her she'd slept a solid eight hours, and the late-afternoon sun streaming across her bed confirmed it.

She might have slept, but she didn't feel particularly rested. Not considering the way things had ended with Mason.

Water was still running.

Frowning, she sat up and listened harder.

And then she realized *what* she was hearing, and she bounded off the bed and out into the hallway. The door to Mason's bathroom was shut, but a very fine wisp of steam was coming out from beneath it.

She knocked on the door. "Mason? What are you doing?"

He didn't answer.

She knew he was chomping at the bit for a shower. But surely he wouldn't have attempted such a thing with his casts. Would he?

It was much too easy to believe that he would.

She knocked on the door again. Harder this time. "Mason!"

Still no answer.

Visions of him knocking himself out on the cast-iron tub quickly filled her mind, and she turned the knob. The door swung open, and a thick waft of steam rolled out.

It also rolled above and around the edges of the shower curtain that was pulled around the deep, old-fashioned tub that she'd bought at an auction and had refinished at a restoration place in Cheyenne.

She grabbed the edge of the curtain, her worry far exceeding her discretion, and she pulled it back.

She got a glimpse of tight, male backside, a scarred back and slick water-darkened hair as the man—half covered in plastic bags, she realized—jerked around to face her, swearing vividly. "Dammit, Court!" He grabbed the shower curtain with almost amusing modesty and pulled it against him. "What the hell?"

She was a nurse, for pity's sake. She was not going

to blush over the sight of a plastic-wrapped, casted-up naked man.

Even *this* naked man.

"That should be my line," she said tartly and reached around him to shut off the water, unintentionally brushing her arm against a warm, wet thigh in her way. They both seemed to jump a little, though Mason couldn't do much, considering he was standing one-footed in the tub while his garbage-bag-shrouded leg was propped on the opposite side of the tub. "If you get either one of those casts wet, you'll be spending even more time at the hospital."

She snatched a thick brown towel off the towel rack. "You're worse than a child," she muttered. "Turn my back for a minute and look what you get up to." She ran the towel over his chest and shoulder, down to the edge of the plastic that he'd taped—with duct tape, yet—around his arm, above the edge of the fiberglass cast. She dried the plastic, hoping furiously that water hadn't leaked beneath it.

"I'm not a freaking child," he snapped and grabbed the towel with his free hand.

Considering that she was facing down all six-five of his bare flesh, she was reminded with excruciating clarity of that particular fact.

And even though they'd slept together, the sight of him took her breath away. Not just because of the mass of perfectly formed sinew and muscle or the remains of bruising that outlined his ribs and extended all the way over his corrugated abdomen, but because of the network of faint scars that webbed across his shoulders and back.

She hadn't seen them before.

The night they'd spent together was indelibly etched

in her mind. Also etched was the fact that they'd spent that night in her bedroom. Her darkened bedroom.

She'd never turned on a light, and he hadn't asked her to.

Given the glare on his face, she had a suspicion that she now knew why.

She forced herself to focus on the most immediate concern—that of his casts remaining dry. Her quickness kept him off guard and allowed her to grab the towel back from him and whip it around his hips. "Hold it there if you want to preserve your dignity."

He grabbed the towel at his hip. "What dignity?" His teeth snapped off the words.

She didn't look at him as she grabbed a second towel from the rack and ran it down the garbage bag taped around his thigh. "If you were so desperate for a shower, you could have asked me for help."

"I don't *want* help," he reminded.

"Just mine, or anyone's?" She didn't wait for an answer as she leaned over the side of the deep tub to reach his plastic-encased foot. "How long have you been in here, anyway?" It had to have been a while to build up as much steam as there'd been. Steam that was now dissipating but had still managed to make her T-shirt feel like it was clinging moistly to her torso.

It was also a miracle he hadn't lost his balance, standing virtually one-footed the way he was.

She straightened and managed by sheer grit not to let her gaze linger on him along the way. Instead, she focused on his face and the cool fury of his green eyes. "Since you managed to get yourself in there, I suppose you can manage to get yourself out." She glanced at the pile of clothes heaped on the floor. He'd obviously been more successful at getting out of his jeans on his own than he'd been in getting into them.

Without letting herself think about it, she scooped them up and carried them out of the bathroom. In his room—no, it was her future baby's room, she reminded herself, only on loan to Mason for the moment—she dropped the clothes in the basket she'd placed in his closet to use as a hamper and then yanked open the dresser drawers and randomly snatched out a set of clean items. She laid them on the side of the bed and sat down beside them to wait.

It took a solid ten minutes.

Ten minutes that crept by with painful slowness while she fought the urge to go and offer him assistance. Her ears were attuned for the slightest sound that he was struggling.

But all she heard was an occasional barely muffled oath, the closing of the bathroom door, which she'd left open, and the rush of water again. Not the shower, though. She could tell.

So she waited. And waited some more.

When he finally appeared, the towel was tucked tightly around his hips, though it separated over the bulge of his plastic-encased cast when he swung on his crutches through the doorway.

His gaze went from her to the clothes and she could see his lips tighten.

"I know you hate needing my help," she said bluntly. "But for now, you're just going to have to live with it." She took a breath. "Or find someone else to help you with your care that you *can* tolerate."

His brows pulled together. "I never said I couldn't tolerate you. Do you want me to leave? Money not worth the hassle, after all?"

"No!" She cleared her throat and reminded herself to be calm. Patient. "I'm not saying that at all. Mason, it's going to be a month before you'll get that cast off your arm, and another few weeks after that before there's even any hope for removing the one on your leg. If this is going to work, I need you to stop fighting me every step of the way, or that time is going to be a nightmare." She rubbed her damp palms down the sides of her cotton pants and pushed to her feet. "It's partly my fault, I know. Nobody likes people prying into their lives, and for that I'm sorry. Your business is your business, and from now on, you have my word that I'll respect that. We need to work together, and that's just as much my responsibility as it is yours."

He exhaled noisily, raising his casted arm, which would have looked comical in its silver duct tape and dark green garbage bag, if she'd been feeling at all humorous. "Stop. Just stop."

Her lips pressed together.

"I don't need you apologizing because I'm a bastard."

"I never said that!"

"I said it." His voice was flat. "I need your help. I don't want to need your help. Or anyone's help. With you it's a double-edged sword, though. And don't bother pretending that you don't understand why."

A wary nervousness jabbed through her insides. "Because we...slept together."

"We didn't sleep." His gaze flicked to the bed beside her. "We crawled inside each other's skin that night."

The nervous jab turned warm and slippery.

"I told you, I wasn't going to be able to forget. To pretend it never happened. It did."

Her breath ran short. She felt as if he were pulling her into the intensity of his gaze.

"The problem is…" His voice was low. Deep. "I can't make myself stop wanting it to happen again."

Her knees actually felt wobbly.

"But you have your future planned out—baby and all. And I've got a career to get back to. So you and I… we're not going there again. It's a bad idea, no matter which way you turn it."

"Oh?" She shook herself a little. "Right. You're right. We're not. Going there." She moistened her lips. "Bad idea. Bad. Bad idea."

"Then let's just stick to the necessities." His lips twisted. "And I'll try to be the least pain in your neck that I can be."

"You're not a pain in the neck. Or," she added swiftly when she saw his expression, "anywhere else. We'll just agree to both remember what we're doing this for."

He gave a short nod.

She let out a quick breath. "Okay. So I have just one more question."

His brows pulled together. "What?"

"Did you use up all the duct tape and garbage bags I had in the garage?"

He looked vaguely startled. Then his lips tilted a little. "There's some tape left on the roll. But you'll be needing more bags."

"Good to know." She picked up his gray soft-knit boxers. "Ready?"

He grimaced, but he moved over to the side of the bed and awkwardly sat down. "As ready as I'm ever going to be, I guess."

Chapter Eight

"Well?" Lisa Pope plopped down onto the chair next to Courtney's. "How are things going with your Mr. Hyde?"

Courtney eyed her coworker. "The same way they've been going in the month since he arrived," she said blithely.

She didn't feel blithe, though.

Since the morning four weeks earlier when he'd insisted he was no hero, they'd both been very careful not to forget the rules of their arrangement.

In one sense, it was working admirably. They'd fallen into a fairly comfortable routine that had involved no more disasters like broken casts. When she got off shift in the morning, they shared breakfast together. Then she'd help him shower, when he was insistent about it—fortunately, his garbage-bag-and-duct-tape method had been effective enough to repeat—and dress, and then she'd catch her "night's" sleep while he entertained himself and often Plato, too.

Her dog had become thoroughly enamored of Mason. Probably because Mason had the patience to sit on her back deck for hours on end, throwing a tennis ball for the big dog to chase around and retrieve.

Then she'd slip in running a couple miles, come back to shower and fix them another meal, and take herself off to work again.

As simple and straightforward as they could keep it.

On the other hand, she felt ready to climb right out of her skin at what was feeling decidedly…domestic. Not even the prospect of having a baby was enough to keep her sane.

She'd finally settled on a donor.

Number 37892.

And she had an appointment set in a few weeks with her sister-in-law, Mallory, when she intended to ask if she was willing to be Courtney's obstetrician and help bring her plan to reality.

So far, Mason was still the only other person who knew her plans.

And *they* certainly weren't discussing it these days.

Not when their conversations remained strictly centered around the practical matters of his physical care and living under the same roof.

"Come on," Lisa wheedled, drawing Courtney out of her thoughts. It was nearly five in the morning and their wholly uneventful shift would be ending soon. "Isn't there even a *little* bit of…flirting? He's single. You're single. You're living together and everyone in the hospital knows that you were kissing outside the imaging suite after he first got to town."

Courtney smiled tightly. "That was a month ago," she

reminded Lisa. Wanting to ignore that particular event had proven to be fruitless when everyone in the hospital, and beyond, seemed to be in the know.

She'd hoped that it would die down, when there'd been no additional fuel added to the fire, but that was evidently a futile hope.

"Well, then what *do* you do while you're spending all those hours together?"

Courtney could have laughed. "We don't spend hours together, exactly." Then she shrugged. "He reads a lot. And I know Axel comes around pretty often when I'm not there." She had even begun suspecting that the two men were talking business, but she hadn't asked. Mason's recovery was continuing fairly smoothly, and that's the only thing she let herself focus on.

She looked at her watch, but the hands still seemed to be crawling around the numbers. "I'll be bringing him in to see Dr. Jackman in a few days to get the cast on his arm removed." Assuming that Mason could manage to wait that long, since she wouldn't put it past him to saw the thing off himself. If he were more dexterous with his left hand, she'd have been seriously worried he'd try to do just that.

As it was, she had no tools in her garage that he could use to that end, and she'd made Axel promise not to provide any if he were asked.

"That'll be good," Lisa was saying. "He'll be able to do a lot more for himself then."

Courtney stared at the duty schedule in front of her. "Mmm-hmm."

And when Mason was able to do more for himself, she couldn't help wondering if he'd decide to leave even before his leg cast came off. He'd still have difficulty managing some tasks, considering the unwieldiness of the cast, but at least he'd have both his arms usable again.

"Something wrong with the schedule?"

"What?" She glanced at Lisa. "Oh. No. Why?"

"You were frowning at it."

"Was I?" She pushed away from the desk and went around it to stare out the sliding doors. "I wonder if it'll snow soon."

"Hope it doesn't before Halloween," Lisa remarked. "Annie's going to be annoyed if her horse costume is covered up too much by a coat."

Courtney smiled. Lisa's six-year-old, Annie, was positively horse crazy. "Even if it is, there's always the fall festival the day before." The community event that included games and costumes, dinner and dancing was held every year in the high school gymnasium.

"Are you going?"

Courtney was scheduled to work the night of Halloween, but not the evening of the festival. "Hadn't thought about it," she lied.

The truth was, she'd thought about it a lot. Had thought about whether or not she should mention it to Mason. And now, with less than a week remaining before it was to be held, it loomed over her larger than ever.

She wished she'd just brought it up to him a few weeks ago. Then it would have seemed a casual mention. Something for him to do if he were interested, to break the monotony of the days. And if he wasn't interested, no big deal. She'd go herself, anyway, because she'd promised her niece Chloe that she'd make an appearance at some point.

"Hey." Wyatt walked through the doors and gave her a curious look as he began pulling off his jacket. "Why're you just standing there?"

"She's mooning over Mason," Lisa said.

Courtney whirled. "I am not!"

Her coworker just grinned wickedly. "You're sure sounding defensive."

It was true, but Courtney rolled her eyes anyway. "You guys need more things to do," she said. "Your imaginations obviously don't have enough occupying them." She nodded toward Wyatt. "Maybe you'd do better asking him how his date with Dee went."

Lisa's eyebrows shot up and she immediately looked at the other nurse. "Well, well. When did this happen and why didn't I know about it? Where'd you go? What'd you do? Are you taking her out again?"

Happy that the other woman's attention was so easily diverted, Courtney went back to the nurse's lounge and signed out. She collected her jacket and purse and quickly left before Lisa could waylay her with more questions.

It was still dark outside, and the air was cold and biting as she climbed into her car. The drive to her house was short—never giving the vehicle's heater a chance to catch up.

The light over her front door was burning. Mason always turned it on before she got home.

Now that the weather was turning colder, she parked her car in the separate garage located next to her backyard, instead of parking in the driveway close to the front door, and went in through the rear kitchen door.

Plato was sitting on the other side of the door, waiting to greet her.

She dumped her purse and jacket on the table and crouched down next to the dog, rubbing his head. She knew once he'd had a few pats from her, he'd trot right on back to Mason's room. He'd considered the bed in there his before Mason had arrived, and nothing since then had changed. If anything, her dog seemed to be more interested in attention from Mason than from her. "You're a good boy," she whispered to the dog, and straightened.

A roll of duct tape was sitting on the counter.

She smiled a little. Mason's unspoken code that he wasn't going to wait another day to be allowed another shower.

When it came to that process, they'd worked out a system there, too, though mostly it involved her sitting outside the shower curtain, pouring shampoo into his hand when he needed it, trying not to offer too much assistance and hiding the fact that the entire event kept her nerves honed to a painfully fine edge.

Just thinking about it made her edgy now, too, and she picked up the plastic-wrapped sandwich that sat on the counter next to the tape and unwrapped it as she padded into the dining room. She sat down in front of the computer and navigated to the cryobank website as she chewed the sandwich. Peanut butter and strawberry jam.

Mason had taken to leaving her sandwiches. He said it was just to prove to her that he wasn't incapable of feeding himself.

Maybe it was true.

The website loaded, and by force of habit, she pulled up the anonymous donor she'd chosen. "Hello, 37892," she whispered. "How are you this morning? We're going to make a baby soon."

Plato, evidently satisfied that she was in for the night, padded out of the dining room and disappeared down the dark hallway.

She propped her chin on her hand and stared at the screen.

The familiar spark of excitement when she thought of her plan to have a family was there. She knew what she wanted and, in her usual way, was going to make it happen.

And if that spark wasn't quite as bright as it ordinarily was, it was simply because the fantasy of it was becoming a reality. And with reality came worries.

Mason and his "devil's advocate" comments hadn't given her anything new to think about. But the closer her plan got to fruition, the more she did think about them.

More accurately, the harder it was to remember that becoming a mother was the bottom line. Not the method in which that occurred.

Nothing had changed since she'd decided on this plan of action.

Nothing except Mason coming back into your life.

She shushed the taunting little voice. Mason wasn't back *in* her life. For that matter, he'd never been in her life.

A one-night stand didn't qualify as "in," after all.

And what they were doing now was a business arrangement. Also not "in."

Plato padded back into the room and propped his head on her knee, whining a little.

She rubbed his head. "What's the matter?"

He turned and headed down the hall, stopping midway to look back at her with another soft whine.

Frowning, she followed him, turning on the hall light as she went.

Mason's bedroom was dark, but there was enough light from behind her to see where he lay on the bed.

"Mason?" she called his name softly, not wanting to wake him if he were asleep. "You all right?"

He didn't answer, and she looked down at the dog by her side. Plato was still whining softly.

"Shh." She slipped her fingers under his collar and nudged him slightly toward her bedroom. "You can sleep with me for a while."

"Wait."

The voice was almost soundless.

Alarm exploded inside her, and she went into Mason's room. When she reached the bed, she could see that his eyes were indeed open. And that his hand was clenched in a fist. "Mason? What's wrong?"

"Back." A low oath came out of his clenched teeth. "Spasm."

She gingerly touched his shoulder. He was so tense, it was like touching a brick wall. "How long have you been like this?"

"Forever." He gave a half-groaning laugh, then just groaned. "A few hours. *Damn* it."

"Can you roll over? I can try some gentle massage. See if it helps."

"I don't think I can move," he muttered.

She had a good idea what the admission cost him. "I can turn you, but I won't if you don't want me to."

"I don't care if you hit me over the head with a sledge-hammer and knock me out."

She toed off her clogs and pressed one knee against the mattress, carefully moving his bed pillows out of the way. "I'm going to move your arms above your head. Slow and easy, okay?" She situated his cast where she wanted it so that it wouldn't get in my way, and when he didn't protest that he felt more pain, she slid one hand beneath his casted thigh and worked her other beneath his shoulders. Ordinarily, she would have turned him toward her, but he was too close to the side of the bed, and there was no room for her to stand on the other side. So she rolled him slowly, gently, away from her until he was on his side. "Okay so far?"

"No worse." His voice was muffled. "This is what I get for flushing the damn pills."

She didn't have to guess which pills he meant. "They wouldn't have stopped a muscle spasm," she reminded calmly.

"But at least I wouldn't have cared when I was having one." He gave a short, rusty-sounding laugh. "That's a joke."

"I figured."

"Good." He let out a long breath, and then she felt him rolling on his own until he was facedown on the mattress. "I don't want you worrying that I'm on the edge of relapsing."

"I wasn't." She was familiar with the signs, and he didn't show any of them. He hadn't ever, really, not even when he'd first arrived and his pain had been constant. She climbed on the bed next to him, kneeling beside his hip. "Your leg comfortable enough?" The angle of the cast didn't exactly promote lying facedown.

"I'll live."

She moistened her lips. Her hands hovered over him, just above the waistband of his dark gray sweatpants. "Where's the pain?"

"Everyfreakingwhere. Either do your voodoo or shoot me in the head."

"Oh, Mason." She settled her hands gently against the small of his back. "I don't suppose you'd be willing for me to cut off your shirt." She didn't want to cause him more pain by trying to get it off over his head.

"I'm not wasting a perfectly good shirt."

"How frugal of you." It was easier to keep talking, because then she wouldn't be *thinking* so much about what she was doing.

Her fingertips lightly explored the contours of his back, searching out the areas of tenderness through the cotton knit. It was pretty easy to find the muscle that was cramping. It was hard as a rock beneath the warmth of his skin. Plus, he ground out a curse and stiffened up when she began working around it.

"This would be easier without the shirt." And with some massage lotion. "Your scars don't bother me, in case that's what you're thinking. I'm a nurse."

"So was my ex-wife. They sure as hell bothered her."

She was so surprised by the admission that her hands stopped moving for a moment. Aside from the one time that he'd mentioned he'd been married, he hadn't referred to it again. She hadn't had the nerve to ask, since it was clearly outside the bounds of their arrangement. She viciously chewed back the questions that rose in her—how'd they meet? How long were they together?

Did he still carry a torch for her?

Was that why his emotions were off-limits?

"I'm not your ex-wife," was all she said. She shifted slightly, gradually applying more pressure along his spine in response to the muscles she could feel slowly loosening under her fingers.

"So I'm learning."

She closed her eyes for a moment, not sure how to take that. "How often does your back get like this?"

She could feel him breathing carefully as she worked. "Happens if I lie around too much. Don't get enough exercise."

"What kind of exercise?"

"Chasing bad guys." His voice turned short.

She swallowed. Chasing them, or being run down by them? She decided to change the subject. "I, um, I confirmed your appointment day after tomorrow to get your arm done."

"Good."

She put a little more of her weight behind her slow, smooth strokes. "If you're getting cabin fever and want to get out a little, Weaver has a fall festival on Saturday. It's a fancy term for a Halloween carnival, but there's food and music and…stuff."

"Ax told me about it."

Of course. She didn't know why she hadn't thought her cousin would mention it. Axel's wife was one of the local business owners who helped sponsor it.

"You gonna do another kissing booth?"

She was glad his face was turned away from her. "That was just that one time. To, um, to raise money for the school."

"I remember the line around your booth. You must've raised a lot."

She had, and had earned herself a lot of ribbing from her family as a result. "The *event* did."

"But the thing this weekend isn't a fundraiser?"

"Nope. Just a community event. People dress up in costumes if they like. They've held it every year since I can remember."

"What're you dressing up as?"

"I hadn't thought about it." The only thing she'd thought about was whether or not Mason would want to go. And if he'd think she was being too *personal* by asking him.

"Think you should go as an angel," he murmured. "My back is actually starting to feel better."

She snorted softly. "That doesn't make me angel material."

"Putting up with me does."

She moistened her lips. "You're not so bad," she managed lightly. "No matter what you think." She was well aware that he hadn't said whether or not he was interested in going. Which she was smart enough to realize meant he was not.

"Why'd you invite me to your apartment that night?"

He couldn't have shocked her more if he'd tried. She stared at the back of his head. "Why'd you show up when I did?" she asked without thought.

"I'm a man." His voice was dry.

She took her cue from that. "And I'm a woman. You think men are the only ones ruled by their sex drives?"

"Generally speaking? Yeah." He turned his head, and she could feel the weight of his hooded gaze. "I know you weren't intending to get pregnant then. We used condoms."

Her face felt like it was on fire. "The last thing on my mind then was having a baby."

"Your brother was still missing then, wasn't he?"

"Mmm-hmm." She focused on his back, working a little harder.

"And then he gets back, and you suddenly decide you want a baby."

"Not exactly. But I will admit that his return helped cement my belief that a person shouldn't necessarily wait for those things in life that they really want." The cotton knit of his T-shirt kept bunching beneath her hands. And she *wanted* to tear it off, and not just because it was hindering her massage, but because her hands simply ached to touch his bare skin.

As if he could hear her thoughts and wanted to put

an end to them, he suddenly rolled onto his back, proving that, not only had she managed to tame the muscle spasm, but he'd become much more agile over the past weeks than she knew.

Which would make her even less of a necessity to him now.

"I guess you're feeling a little better." She brushed her hands together and scooted to the side of the bed, but his hand latched around her wrist, halting her.

Electricity shot through her. "What?"

Almost as soon as he'd grabbed her, he released her. "Nothing." His voice was gruff. "Just…thanks."

She chewed the inside of her lip. Pushed off the bed and felt around with her feet for her clogs. "That's what I'm here for."

"You looking forward to having your place back to yourself? Start turning this room into a nursery?"

Just nod and agree. How hard was that?

"Looking forward to the nursery? Yes. Looking forward to you leaving?" She finally found the shoes. "Surprisingly, not so much." Then, before her unwise tongue could get her into even more trouble, she hurried out of the room.

She closed herself in her bedroom and leaned back against the door. "Stupid, Courtney," she whispered. Just plain stupid.

And then she saw the box sitting on her bed.

It was small. And it was wrapped—rather unevenly— in brown paper. The same kind of paper as the bags at the grocery store where she shopped.

She went over to the box and picked it up. There was no tag. No label.

Shaking it lightly gave her no hint of what was inside and she slid her finger beneath the tape, pulling off the paper wrapping. The box it covered was plain white, also offering no hint.

Inside her chest, her heart skittered around. She lifted the lid off the box.

Her knees went loose and weak and she plopped down on the bed, staring at the silver rattle that was nestled snugly among the padding inside the box. She held it up.

It had been engraved. *Mommy's little angel.*

Her hand trembled and the rattle jingled softly.

Without thought, she left her room again and went into Mason's. Still holding the rattle, she sat down on the bed beside him.

"I don't care if it is a bad idea." Before her mind could stop what her heart wanted, she leaned over and pressed her mouth to his.

Stars might as well have exploded inside her chest for the sensation that streaked through her. She lifted her head, catching her breath, but his hand came up, sinking through her hair, pulling her back to him.

The rattle slid from her nerveless fingers when his mouth opened against hers. She felt herself sinking deeper into him and tore her mouth away. She pushed her hand against his chest, resisting even though the last thing she wanted to do was resist. "Tell me what to do about you," she whispered. "You want to keep me at a distance, and then you do this?" She jiggled the rattle and it rang musically between them. "You, who doesn't even approve of my plan?"

"You put the rattle on that wish list."

She laughed a little brokenly. "And obviously, you've been poking around on the websites I happen to visit on the internet. I ought to be angry. I would never have even realized you've been spying, except you go and announce it by putting a box on my bed! What am I supposed to make of this?"

"It's just a gift. And there's no spying involved, considering how you never seem to close a browser window."

His fingers were still threaded through her hair, and she lowered her forehead to his chin. She pulled in a long, slow breath. Let it out even more slowly. "Nothing with you is ever *just*."

"I didn't give it expecting something in return."

"Something." She lifted her head. Peered into his face. "Like me throwing myself at you again?"

"You never threw yourself at me."

"What would you call it then?"

His fingers slid along her neck. It took far more control than she possessed not to shiver. "A night of miracles," he murmured.

Her throat tightened. "Be careful," she warned, much more for her own benefit than his. "That sounded unabashedly romantic."

"That the knockout young nurse could see past a face that scares children?"

Her chest squeezed. He really meant it. "I don't think it's the scar that scares anyone." She ran her finger down the jagged mark that slashed his face. "It's the fact that you have a very fierce glower when you try." She laid her palm against his cheek. "But you smiled at me when you paid for your kiss." And she'd been sunk.

He wasn't smiling now, though. If anything, he looked…regretful.

He caught her hand in his. "You should go to bed."

She lifted her eyebrows, even though her stomach was sinking. "I'm guessing that's not an invitation." She didn't wait for the obvious answer and sat up, sliding off the bed. She lifted the rattle. "It's a beautiful gift, Mason. But it's much too extravagant." That's why she hadn't ordered it herself. Because she couldn't quite justify the cost.

"It's a gift." His words were clipped. "You're not supposed to worry about the expense."

"But—"

"I can afford it, okay? Just because I'm not currently the picture of gainful employment doesn't mean I'm broke."

"That never occurred to me." She shook her head. "I...we're getting off track." The last thing she wanted to do was offend him. She turned the rattle between her fingers. "Let me try again. Thank you, Mason, for the very thoughtful gift. I'll cherish it always."

"You mean, the baby will."

She smiled sadly. "No. I mean *I* will." And then, before she could forget herself yet again where he was concerned, she went to her bedroom and closed the door.

She held the rattle cradled against her chest and sighed.

Chapter Nine

"Mason looks like he's enjoying himself." Courtney's cousin-in-law Tara slipped into the folding chair beside her at one of the round tables that the family had commandeered at the fall festival. Courtney looked over to where Mason was propped on his crutches among her cousins and her brother. He had his newly cast-free hand wrapped around a beer, and a grin on his face.

"I think he's so glad to get out of one of his casts that he'd enjoy most anything." She smiled a little wryly.

Until that morning, she'd believed that Mason had no intentions of coming to the festival. But when she'd gotten off duty from the hospital, he'd been up waiting for her and had asked what time the "thing" was.

She'd been nearly stunned stupid before she'd stammered out the time.

Then, when she'd gone to her room to grab some sleep, she'd just laid there staring at the ceiling.

"Well, now that he's obviously getting out and about more, maybe you can get him to Sunday dinner."

Courtney stifled a sigh and lifted her shoulder. "Maybe." Every week, someone in the family put on a big Sunday dinner for whoever could come. Since Mason had arrived, Courtney had missed all but one, and he'd flatly refused to "intrude," even though she'd assured him he wouldn't be doing any such thing.

Mostly, she figured he'd had enough of her family en masse when they'd gone to her parents' for dinner that one night.

"D'you ever think you can figure a man out?" Realizing she'd spoken the question aloud when Tara gave her an amused look, Courtney felt her skin turn warm. "Rhetorical question," she said quickly.

Tara didn't take it rhetorically, though. She looked over at the men again. "As much as a man can figure out a woman," she said. Her gaze slid to Courtney. "It helps when you can both talk to each other about what's going on inside."

Courtney couldn't help making a face at that. "Some men are better at that than others, I'd think."

"So are some women," Tara pointed out. "My personal take? When you can allow yourself to start trusting the other person not to hurt you the way you expect… or fear…then amazing things can happen." She smiled gently. "Even coming to understand what makes that particular man tick. And understanding even better what makes you tick."

Courtney propped her chin on her hand. "I know what makes me tick," she murmured. "Family."

"A true Clay," Tara said. "Think that's pretty consistent among all of you."

"You're one of us now, too."

Tara's gaze looked past Courtney toward the men. She smiled, and there was such a contented satisfaction in that smile, Courtney felt a little envious.

"I still have to pinch myself sometimes," Tara admitted. "My parents are gone, though I have my brother, of course. But your family is particularly tight. I'm not sure if all of you realize how unique that can be since it's the way it's always been for you."

"I don't know about unique, but I do know that I can't imagine *not* having the family I have." Courtney looked at Mason. "It's one of the reasons I never wanted to move away from Weaver. I can't imagine growing up without that particular bedrock. We're lucky, I know." Then she grinned. "Even during those times when I wish—for a moment—to have just a little more privacy."

Tara laughed. "I have to admit there are a few times when I've thought the same thing." Her eyes danced. "Particularly when the boys drop by unannounced to play pool with Axel." She pushed her chair back and stood. She was wearing a floor-length, royal blue velvet gown, with a sword strapped around her hip. She looked like a petite character out of Narnia. "Come on. I haven't seen you dance once yet this evening, and you're usually the belle of the ball. Get that man you can't stop looking at out on the dance floor."

"I'm pretty sure Mason doesn't want to attempt dancing while his leg is in a cast." Or any other time. Not with her, at any rate.

If he did, he'd have asked her.

That she did know about him.

Tara lifted her brows, as if she could read exactly what was in Courtney's thoughts. "Then dance with someone else," she suggested pointedly. "It's not like you haven't been asked a dozen times already."

That was true enough. Courtney had turned down all the offers, though, because the only arms she was interested in holding her belonged to her enigmatic boarder.

"Good point." She pushed to her feet, too, and tugged down the thigh-length tunic of her orange-and-red clown costume. She glanced around, spotted a good target and made her way across the room in her long-toed red shoes. When she reached Wyatt Mead, where he was hovering against the wall near the door, she grabbed his hand. "Come and dance with me."

He looked horrified. "I don't even know how."

"You owe me," she reminded. "You can escape later."

"I wasn't planning to escape," he huffed.

"Please." She pulled him toward the dance floor. "You were just about ready to slide out the door." She turned toward him and held up her arms. "You can either put your arms around me, or we can stand here looking like idiots."

He looked even more horrified and grabbed her hand in his. He put his other hand on her waist, and they began shuffling around the crowded dance area. His only concession to a costume was the wildly colored, spinning bow tie he wore with his flannel shirt and jeans.

"Don't worry," Courtney told him in a low voice. "Dee is watching every move."

"What?"

"Why haven't you asked her to dance?"

"Because I don't know *how* to dance," he reminded.

Without any effort, she managed to guide them a little closer to Dee. Plus, she could see Mason over Wyatt's shoulder. "Seems like you're dancing well enough to me."

She could practically hear him grinding his teeth. "What do you women want, anyway?"

She almost laughed. "We want the men we're interested in to be interested back."

He frowned. "How can she not know I'm interested? We went out on a date!"

"Did you ask her for another one?"

"Well, not yet, but—"

"Why not?"

"She's been busy. They're doing all sorts of special stuff over at the school these days."

"Doesn't matter," Courtney advised. "Busy or not, she wants to know you want her. For Pete's sake, Wyatt. She's not so busy that she didn't come tonight. And as far as I can tell, she hasn't taken her eyes off you." For that matter, the other woman was presently glaring daggers at Courtney. "At least *ask*."

The fact that she was advising Wyatt to do what she herself refused to do was not lost on her.

But she'd known both Wyatt and Dee for years. Nudging them together was perfectly logical when she knew how they both felt.

Pushing herself toward Mason when she didn't have a clue what he felt was another matter entirely. And besides, what was the point of trying to engage Mason in something that would only end sooner rather than later?

She had plans.

So did he.

And those plans weren't exactly on intersecting paths.

The only thing they had that could conceivably intersect was chemistry.

Good, old-fashioned S.E.X.

She realized the song was winding down and stepped

away from Wyatt. "Go on," she insisted. "Better to ask and get shot down than not ask and never know."

She watched him only long enough to see him pull in a deep breath and take a step toward the side of the gymnasium where Dee was sitting.

Then she turned.

Her gaze collided with Mason's from across the room.

Her stomach dipped and swayed, but she set off toward him, marching her way around and through the crowd in her silly clown shoes until she stopped next to him. Her eyes were on him, though her smile included her brother and her cousin Casey, who were standing there with him. "Having fun?"

"Having fun watching you try to walk in those big ol' shoes," Casey drawled. "You're never gonna snag a man looking like that, honey."

Courtney gave her cousin a kind look. "And you're never gonna snag a woman, Casey, unless you figure out how to open your mouth without inserting your foot in it."

Ryan chuckled and slid his arm around Courtney's shoulders. "Case is just jealous," he said, "because he knows all you have to do is crook your little finger and guys come running from miles away. He, on the other hand, hasn't had a pretty girl look his way all night."

"Women are too much trouble," Casey groused, though his gray eyes were full of goading laughter. He took a pull on his beer. "Give her an inch, and she'll wanna take a mile."

"And a man like you is any different?" Courtney shook her head. Her handsome cousin was twenty-eight and showed no sign of wanting to settle down. Which was not to say that he didn't enjoy his share of female company. As long as it didn't last past a night or two.

She looked at Mason and, ignoring the dancing nerves in her stomach, gestured toward the dance floor. "Do you want to give it a try?" It was an effort, but she managed to keep her voice light. "I can be your human crutch."

His brows pulled together slightly. "Then I'll be the one looking like a clown."

Even though she'd expected him to turn her down, her disappointment didn't feel any less acute. "Never hurts to ask," she dismissed blithely. "Ryan, how about you?"

"Since my wife abandoned me to deliver a baby and my daughter prefers the company of the games over there—" he jerked his chin toward the side of the room that was set up with carnival-style games "—might as well."

Courtney rolled her eyes. "So good for my ego." But she was smiling as she headed out to the dance area and turned to her brother, because it still struck her as a miracle that he was around at all.

He smoothly swept her into a two-step. "How's it going with Hyde?"

"Fine."

He smiled faintly. "Okay. Now, how's it *really* going with Hyde?"

"Fine," she insisted.

"What about the two of you playing tonsil hockey at the hospital?"

"We most certainly weren't doing anything of the sort!"

He raised his eyebrow.

She huffed. "First of all, that was weeks ago. Second, you know what gossip is like in this town. Things get blown completely out of proportion."

"I can always tell when you're lying."

She exhaled noisily. "I'm not lying! Admittedly, he's not the perfect patient, but he's come a long way in the time he's been here."

"So, you're telling me that the only thing going on under your roof is the nurse-patient deal?"

She swallowed. "That's all." And that, sad to say, *was* the truth.

"Then why," he asked in a low voice, "did he have Axel drive him to the drugstore yesterday, where he bought a box of condoms?"

She stumbled over her own bright red clown shoes. "I have no idea," she said faintly. "Maybe you should ask him."

Her brother's eyes were narrowed, obviously unconvinced. "Maybe I will," he said.

She cleared her throat, desperate to change the subject. "So, um, when I was watching Chloe for you last weekend, she told me she's decided it's time you and her mom give her a baby brother or sister."

"She's been on that kick for a while now."

"And…? It's not like you're getting any younger, brother dear."

"No," a woman's laughing voice said from behind her, "but he just keeps getting better."

Startled, Courtney turned to see her sister-in-law ready to cut in and could have wept with relief. "How'd the delivery go?"

"False alarm." Mallory smiled. She was still dressed in pale blue scrubs. "Just some strong Braxton Hicks contractions, as Mom kept trying to convince Dad, but he was convinced that she was in true labor. Poor guy is out of his mind worrying about his wife." She raised her eyebrows. "Mind if I cut in?"

"Please," Courtney offered, as she stepped away from her brother. "He keeps stepping on my clown toes."

"Hard not to when they're about six inches too long," he defended himself as he swept his wife into a close hold.

Courtney moved away, with the sound of Mallory's soft laughter in her ears.

Mason had bought *condoms?*

She was afraid to assume that he meant to use them with her.

Everywhere she looked, she saw couples. Families.

Thoroughly agitated, she collected her purse from their unoccupied table and headed toward Mason again. Dinner was long over, and the only things left for the night were more carnival games for the children she didn't have and dancing with the partner she didn't have.

The non-partner who'd bought condoms.

She stopped next to him. "Do you want to stay longer, or are you ready to go?"

He immediately set his beer on the table behind him. He gave her a close look. "What's wrong?"

She shook her head. "Nothing. Do you want to stay or go?"

"Go."

She nodded. "Fine. I'll just say good-night to my folks and meet you by the door." She didn't wait to watch him crutch his way there but looked around to find her parents. They, too, were on the dance floor. She worked her way close enough to wave goodbye, then headed to the main gymnasium doors, where Mason was waiting.

She pushed them open and waited for him to pass through. "I'll bring up the car."

"I can make it to the car."

"Your choice." She headed across the sidewalk toward

the crowded parking lot, digging in her purse for her keys as she went. She could hear the thump-slide-thump of Mason behind her and had to fight off the urge to slow her pace and hover closer to him, lest his crutches catch on an uneven bit of pavement. She reached the car ahead of him and had the back door open and waiting by the time he got there.

Handing her the crutches, he used both—hallelujah—of his arms to lower himself onto the seat and slide across it until his cast was inside the car. Without a word, she handed him the crutches to lay on the floor behind the seats and closed the door, then went around to the driver's side.

In minutes, she was driving out of the parking lot.

"What's bugging you?"

She glanced in the rearview mirror, but the only thing she could make out were the headlights of the car behind her. "Nothing."

"Yeah, right."

She cleared her throat with a soft cough. "Just some gossip I heard."

"About?"

She pulled the car off to the side of the street, shoved it into Park and looked over the seat at him. "About you. Buying condoms!"

"And that has you pissed off?"

Her hands tightened around the steering wheel. "Why do you need to be out buying condoms?"

"Because I couldn't find any in your house."

She gaped. "You've been *looking*?"

"Yes."

His answer was so calm and immediate that she blinked. "What do you plan on doing with them?"

Even in the dim light, she could see his eyebrow

lift. "*If* I plan on doing something, it won't be making X-rated balloons out of them." His voice was mild.

She pressed her fingertips hard against her temples. "*Who* are you planning to use them with?" She dropped her hands. "Maybe you need me to take you to Colbys, so you can pick up some women, too?"

"Don't be stupid."

She stared at him. "Well, what am I supposed to think, Mason? You're practically hands-off for weeks, and you wouldn't even try to dance with me. I get it that you didn't want to dance. Pretty hard to do, with the cast and all, but—"

He leaned forward until his hand could catch behind her neck. "I bought them because of you," he said evenly. "Because I'm not sure how much more my self-control can take." Then, before she could wrap her mind around that, he let go of her and was sitting back again. "How did you even find out, anyway? Axel just dropped me off in front of the store. He doesn't know what the hell I bought."

"This is Weaver," she said faintly. "You can't do anything in this town without somebody taking notice and spreading the word along."

He grimaced. "Nice."

"You said it was a bad idea for us to go down that path."

"And people go down paths they shouldn't all the time. If I'm no better, then I at least want to be prepared. Oh, hell. This is great," he muttered. He'd turned to look out the back window.

Her mouth was dry. A million thoughts were racing through her head, but nothing was coming out of her lips. He was still looking out the back, and her gaze followed his to the flashing red-and-blue lights, but for a moment, even they didn't make sense to her.

And then, when a police officer knocked on the window beside her head, they did.

She groaned and rolled down the window. "Hey there, Dave."

The deputy sheriff cocked his head, eyeing her. "Everything okay, Courtney? You're in a no-parking zone."

"Sorry. I'll move on."

The man nodded, though he gave Mason a long look. "Drive safe," he said and thumped his hand on the top of the car before walking back to his patrol vehicle.

Courtney rolled up her window and put the car in Drive. "I can't believe you bought condoms." She shakily pulled back onto the street.

"Better to be prepared," he said dismissively.

Except she didn't want the subject dismissed. "Because I want a baby, and you want to make sure it's not yours?"

"That's not what I said."

Her hands twisted on the steering wheel. "But it's true, isn't it?"

She heard him sigh. "I can't believe everyone in this freaking town knows everyone else's business," he muttered.

It wasn't a direct response, but it didn't have to be.

She knew the answer.

"Maybe I've changed my mind, too. Maybe I don't want to sleep with you again."

"Then you won't."

How easily he said it. As if it hardly mattered to him one way or the other. Maybe that particular intersection was more in her mind than in reality, after all.

A lump lodged in her throat, and she continued the

drive home in silence. She let him out next to the house and drove back to park in the garage. He'd gone inside by the time she went in through the back door.

There was no sign of Plato. Her dog had fully defected to the enemy.

She toed off the silly clown shoes in the kitchen and padded in her stocking feet through the dining room, then down the hall.

Mason was waiting. There was no mistaking that particular fact. Not with him leaning against the wall, one crutch propped under his arm to help support him.

Plato sat next to him, leaning his big, fluffy body against Mason's cast.

Her heart charged unevenly inside her chest. Because it felt safer, she looked down at her dog and held out her hand. "Have you forgotten who buys your dog food?"

Plato rolled to his feet and came forward, his tail wagging as he sloppily dragged his tongue over her hand. She crouched next to him and rubbed her hands over his coat. His tail flopped harder, and his soft brown eyes looked hearteningly ecstatic. "Yes, you're a handsome boy, even if you do prefer someone else over me."

"He hasn't lost his loyalty to you," Mason assured her. "He just tolerates me 'cause I've tossed him the tennis ball a few times."

"Hmm." The dog sprawled on the floor and rolled over, waiting for his belly to be rubbed. She couldn't help but smile a little at the blatant invitation and complied. "I don't think *tolerate* is quite the word." She pushed to her feet. "He's going to miss you when you leave."

"That sounds more like a reminder to us both that I will be leaving."

"I don't need to remind myself," she said. "I'm aware

of it every…single…day. Just as I am aware that you purchasing a box of condoms doesn't change that." She lifted her chin. "Maybe I don't want anything to change. Maybe I like the fact that you'll be leaving. No strings and all that. It works both ways."

The corner of his lip curled. "I'd bet my last dollar that it doesn't work that way for you."

It didn't, but he didn't have to know that he was right. She did have *some* pride. "I told you before that I wasn't looking for a husband." She spread her hands. "I'm not even looking for a baby-daddy. As you well know, I've got that angle covered with number 37892."

His brows yanked together. "What?"

"Number 37892," she repeated blithely. "That's the donor I've chosen."

"I can't believe you're still going through with this."

"If you thought I wouldn't, why'd you buy that keep-sake rattle?"

"Let me rephrase. I can't believe you still want to have a baby via spermsicle."

She propped her hands on her hips. "We're back to that now? Why shouldn't I?" She waved her hands. "I'm reasonably responsible. I can afford to raise a child if I'm careful, and I have a fabulous family around me for support! I'd rather do this on my own than depend on a man to be with me who doesn't even want to be there in the first place!"

His eyes narrowed. "Are you speaking generally or specifically?"

She huffed. "Neither. For heaven's sake, Mason. Stop worrying. I decided I wanted a baby long before you came back into the picture. Don't want to bash your ego, but you really had nothing whatsoever to do with it. I just realized that for those things you really, *really* want in life, you shouldn't wait. Because you never know what might happen." She gestured at him. "You're a perfect example," she said. "You could have been killed by that SUV. Wasn't there anything in your life that you would have regretted *not* doing, if you hadn't been as lucky as you were?" She made a face. "Oh, that's right. I'm sorry. You're the emotional-island guy. You don't let yourself care about anything else besides your job."

"My job was—is—the only thing that I'm good at." His voice was flat, the scar on his face standing out whitely. "I didn't fail it. And it hasn't failed me."

"Who'd you fail, Mason? Your ex-wife? The one who didn't like your scars? Who didn't hang around to see you conquer your painkiller addiction?"

"Don't waste time analyzing me."

"And don't you waste time thinking that I should wait around for some guy to sweep me off my feet and make my every dream come true," she said swiftly. "I live in Weaver, Mason. I know nearly every guy in this town. If there was someone around who made my bells ring, then I'd be out there ringing 'em, but there's not."

"Weaver's not the only place in the world."

"You think I don't know that? I lived in Cheyenne while I was studying nursing. I've traveled with my parents around the United States. I've traveled abroad with friends. I *choose* Weaver. It's where I grew up, and it's where I want my child to grow up. Everywhere I turn, I am surrounded by family and friends who've found their partners in life. Who've got their metaphorical white picket fence, with babies and all." She lowered her hands finally. "Well, I'm not waiting for a white picket fence that may never come. Maybe you and I aren't so different, after all. You know who and what you are. And

I know who and what I am. They're just on completely different planes."

She took a step back, waiting for her pounding heart to climb down out of her throat. Waiting, too, for him to say something. Anything.

But all he did was stand there, his fist clenched around the handgrip of his crutch, a muscle ticking in his jaw.

Her heart did climb out of her throat then. It slowly sank, heading right for her toes.

"It's late," she finally said huskily. "I'm going to bed." She knew better than to ask if he needed anything before she went.

Because even if he did, he wouldn't ask.

Chapter Ten

She went out on a date.

With Dr. Flannery.

Despite all her claims that she wasn't interested in finding a man, she'd gone out with one.

Mason still couldn't believe it. Not even after he'd watched Courtney—wearing a dress that gave new meaning to little and black—climb into Flannery's low-slung car, parked at the curb.

Mason was inside the house, watching from the window, and *he'd* seen the length of sleek, shapely leg that was exposed when she'd climbed into the sports car. He was pretty damn certain that Pierce Flannery—orthopedic guy that he was—had been studying that perfect limb, too.

And now, they'd been gone for over four hours.

It was nearly midnight, and Mason was about ready to climb out of his skin. What the hell were they doing that it took four hours?

He knew what he'd want to be doing. Same thing he'd been wanting to do from the day he'd seen Courtney again. Same thing that had driven him to buy condoms. Just in case.

The damnable thing was that he'd *had* opportunities. After that rattle business. He'd held her in his arms. She'd even kissed him before he'd pushed her away. And the day of the Halloween shindig. Before she'd found out about his not-so-anonymous purchase and his "just in case" theory had flown out the window.

He should have danced with her.

Even if he'd made an ass out of himself trying, he should have danced.

He shoved his fingers through his hair. It felt odd without the cast, which had been removed the week before, but he was mighty glad to have the thing off even if his arm—paler than the rest of him—looked like some sort of alien thing.

If she hadn't found out about the condoms, would she have still decided to go out with the doctor from Braden?

He grimaced and looked over at Plato, who was taking up nearly as much of the couch cushions as Mason was. "Where the hell are they?"

Plato sighed noisily and flopped his tail twice. His eyebrows seemed to twitch as his gaze went from side to side.

"I know," Mason muttered. "It's none of my damn business. At least that's what *she* would tell me." Grabbing his crutches, he managed to pull himself off the couch. He headed toward the kitchen but stopped at the computer desk in the dining room.

He slid the mouse around, and the swirl of stars on the screen disappeared. Number 37892 stared back at him. Or at least the webpage describing 37892's attributes stared back at him.

Six foot one. 190 pounds. Straight brown hair. Green eyes. A lawyer.

"Probably an ambulance chaser," he muttered and kept moving into the kitchen.

Courtney had left him a plate of food that was ready to go. All he had to do was punch a few numbers on the microwave.

She took the whole room-and-board thing pretty seriously, even if she had come to the realization that he was an ass. And if—*when*—she got home from her date with Dr. Feelgood, she'd expect that plate to be empty or worry why.

So even though his appetite was just as nonexistent as it had been after she'd left, he heated the plate and ate the chicken and rice concoction while standing at the counter. It was easier than trying to carry the plate over to the table and sit down.

When he was finished, he rinsed the plate in the sink, set it in the dishwasher and crutched his way back to the living room. He sat down next to Plato again, where he had a view out the front window through the wide-open plantation shutters.

"Guess we're waiting, Plato."

The dog circled a few times before settling with his head on Mason's knee. The dog sighed hugely.

So did Mason.

"Are you sure I can't talk you into a nightcap?"

Courtney smiled at Pierce and shook her head. She knew the guy was angling for an invitation inside, and she just couldn't make herself pretend she was interested.

Not that the evening had been unpleasant.

Pierce Flannery was an attractive, intelligent and relatively engaging companion. They even had similar interests, not to mention their complementary professions. They'd driven to Gillette for dinner simply because Courtney had happened to mention that she enjoyed Thai food and that was the closest place for it.

By all rights, she should have thoroughly enjoyed herself and been more than happy to extend the evening a little longer.

But encouraging the man wasn't fair.

For that matter, accepting his invitation to dinner hadn't been exactly fair.

Not when she'd agreed only because she wanted to get Mason out from beneath her skin.

Or maybe get underneath Mason's skin, a fact that didn't make her feel any less guilty.

Mason was still burrowed right where he always had been—maybe even further—and if he was bothered in the least by her unexpected date with the eligible doctor, he'd certainly hidden it well.

And now she had managed to encourage a perfectly nice man in whom she had absolutely no interest.

All in all, she felt like the worst sort of slug.

"I'm sure," she told Pierce. "I have an early morning." They were parked at the curb in front of the house, and thanks to the lamp burning in her living room, she could easily see Mason through the front window, sitting on the couch. Despite the late hour, he was up.

Waiting?

Trying hard to ignore that fact, she leaned over the console and quickly kissed Pierce's cheek. "Thank you for dinner. It was very nice."

"I'll call you again."

She sighed a little. Oh, she hated this. "Pierce, you're a really nice man. But I'm just…well, I'm not in a place right now where I'm ready to—"

"Not even for a simple dinner?" His smile was rueful as he looked past her toward the house. He could see Mason just as easily as she had. "Well, it never hurts to ask."

Before she could stop him, he climbed out of the car and came around to her door to open it.

Feeling even worse, she got out, too. "I did have a good time, Pierce."

"But I'm not the right man to be having a good time with," he surmised. He smiled slightly and caught her hand, lifting it to his lips. "Don't look so upset. You know where I am if you change your mind."

She knew she wouldn't, but she still appreciated his kindness. "I do." She stepped back from the curb and watched him walk around his car once more. She tugged her coat more closely around her. "Drive safe."

He sketched a wave and drove away.

She let out a long breath and slowly turned on her heel to face the house. Mason had moved from the couch and was waiting with the front door open. He was barefoot, wearing his cast-altered jeans and a short-sleeved gray T-shirt, and if he was bothered by the definite chill in the November air, he didn't show it.

And just looking at him made something inside her stomach dip and sway.

A part of her wished that would go away.

A larger part of her wished that the sensation would never end.

And wasn't that a fine thing?

Steeling herself, she marched up the walk. "This is your fault," she told him as she stomped past him. She peeled out of her coat and tossed it on a chair. "That was a perfectly nice guy. One I wouldn't have even gone out with if you hadn't driven me to it." Reaching around him, she shut the door with perhaps a little more force than she'd intended.

"If he's such a nice guy, why are you pissed off?"

"Because I don't *want* a nice guy!" Her voice rose. "Foolish me, I just want *you*." Annoyed with herself for admitting it just as much as she was annoyed with him for…well…everything, she kicked off her pumps. They went sailing across the living room, and Plato launched off the couch, catching one of them in his mouth. He brought it back to Courtney, dropping it at her feet. Courtney barely noticed. She hadn't taken her eyes off of Mason. "You went out and bought those darned condoms, but if we end up using any, you're going to hate yourself. And as much as I want you, I don't want to be one more reason for you to do that. Not when it seems you already have enough to beat yourself up over."

He looked pained. "You deserve more than I can give you."

Her annoyance suddenly wavered, which was not a good thing. Because in its place something far more dangerous began taking root. The same thing that had been trying to take root for weeks. The kind of thing that made her forget all the good, logical reasons why his staying with her *was* temporary.

"I'm an adult," she said with as much starch as she could maintain. "And as I have tried to make plain before, I get to decide for myself what I deserve. What I want." She stepped closer, deliberately invading his space. "Or have you forgotten that I am a grown woman?"

The pale green of his eyes seemed to sharpen. "Not

likely. And be careful how hard you poke that stick, Courtney. You might get more than you bargained for."

The fact that she could goad him at all sent sharp-edged excitement skittering through her. She took another step closer. The toes of her bare feet brushed his. "If you weren't concerned about that, why concern yourself with being *prepared?* Why take that little trip to the drugstore?"

"Because I'm a practical man," he said flatly. "And I'm used to covering all the bases. The fact is, I can't be around you for long without wanting to make love to you. Doesn't matter that common sense tells me we're better off not going there."

It was hardly a romantic response.

But it was honest.

And she knew deep in her heart that she'd rather have Mason's honesty than pretty romance from someone else any day of the week.

She tilted her head back, looking up at him. She moistened her lips, but her mouth still felt dry. "Do you want to make love to me now?"

His jaw flexed. If she moved her head an inch, she'd be able to brush her lips against it.

"Don't ask stupid questions."

She inhaled carefully, ruthlessly containing her leaping nerves. "*Will* you make love to me?" She waited a beat. "Now?"

"Courtney—" His hands lifted, then clenched into fists, not touching her. "You're killing me."

"*Will* you?"

"Somebody should have taught you when you were a kid not to play with fire." And then he muttered an oath and pulled her to him.

His mouth covered hers and her senses leapt. She

pressed closer. Her arm knocked into his crutch and it clattered against the wall behind them. His stance wavered and he tore his mouth from hers, swearing again. "This is an accident waiting to happen."

She handed him his crutch again and leaned up to brush her lips over his. "Only while we're standing."

And then she went back down on her bare heels and took a few steps away. She gave him a steady look, even though there was not a single cell inside of her that felt steady. "I know how to solve that." Without giving herself a chance to think about the wisdom of what she was doing, she turned and headed down the hallway.

After a breathless moment, she finally heard the distinct sound of him following.

The relief she felt was nearly crippling. But she went blindly into her bedroom and hadn't even had a chance to pull back the quilt on her bed, when he came in the room. He didn't stop until he stood behind her.

His crutches dropped to the floor, and she started to turn, but his hands closed over her shoulders, staying her. Shivers danced down her spine when he brushed her hair over her shoulder and kissed the back of her neck.

He slid one arm around her waist, his long fingers splaying flat against her belly.

Breathing normally suddenly became a challenge. Because she couldn't help herself, her hand closed over his as if she were afraid he'd let go of her before she was ready.

If she ever was ready.

"You're better at balancing on one foot than I thought."

He made a faint sound. His mouth moved from the nape of her neck along her shoulder, left bare by the boatneck of her dress. "Nearly six weeks of practice."

She didn't want to think about how long it had been. She threaded her fingers through his at her waist and turned within the circle of his arm.

Her breasts brushed against his hard chest, and his body heat seemed to singe through the fabric between them. She wasn't sure if it was her pounding heart or his that vibrated between them. Without thought, her hands moved to his arms. Up over his shoulders to his neck. Her fingers slipped through the unruly length of his dark hair, tugging his head toward hers. *Kiss me.* The demand swirled through her mind, and whether he read her thoughts or understood the urgency behind her grasping hands, his mouth covered hers.

His hands clasped her hips, and he dragged her into him.

And the world whirled.

As if no time had passed at all since that other time when he'd turned her inside out.

One tiny part of her mind scrambled toward sensibility. Toward reason. As much as she wanted him, she couldn't lose herself to him again.

Not completely.

The first time had been difficult enough to recover from. Now…

"Wait." She tore her mouth away from his. Her lips tingled and her voice was raw. Focus on something practical, she thought with near desperation. Focus, and remember that this is only about sex. "The condoms. Are they in your room?"

His hand moved away from her. And then like a magician pulling a coin from out of thin air, he held a square little packet between his fingers. He'd had it in his pocket.

He tossed it on the nightstand, where it landed next to

the base of the lamp that she'd left lit, and put his hands on her again. "What are you wearing under this dress?"

Her brain felt like it was operating in gelatin. "What?"

His lips curved faintly. "Under the dress," he murmured again. He pressed his mouth to her shoulder, and she felt the zipper at the back of her dress suddenly loosen under his nimble fingers. With no effort at all, he nudged the wide collar off her shoulders and down her arms. With no other impediment, the narrow black sheath slipped to the floor at her feet, leaving her clad only in her panties, a strapless bra and the pink jewel in her navel.

"Pink," he murmured. "I keep thinking about you in pink."

She shivered again. For every moment when she felt in control, two more came on its heels when she felt it slipping out of her grasp. She twisted in his arms and stepped out of the dress, kicking it aside. Then she put her hands on the hem of his shirt and dragged it upward. "Off," she said huskily when he tried to stop her—as she'd known he would. "Or you're not going to see anything beneath the pink panties and bra." She met his gaze. "I've seen the scars, remember?"

His eyes narrowed a little. "You've seen everything. More than once," he corrected, "since you won't let a man take a shower in peace. A distinct inequity, if you ask me." Between his dark lashes, his pale eyes seemed to gleam. Then quick as a flash, his hand went behind her, and she felt the clasp of her bra come loose.

Her nipples pulled together even more tightly.

Her chin lifted. She let the bra fall away and was gratified by the slight glazing that seemed to come over his eyes. "When you get your cast off, you can shower in peace all you want," she purred.

Of course, at that point, he wouldn't need her at all.

She kept pulling on the shirt, and finally, he lifted his arms and yanked it off his head. His balance wavered a little, and her arms shot around him.

The contact was blistering and she gasped. Her fingertips curled into the warm, satiny skin stretching up his spine. She only realized that they'd dipped lower, sliding beneath the waist of his jeans, when he gave a laughing curse and grabbed her arms, pushing her gently until her legs hit the mattress.

She tumbled backward, and then he stood over her, balanced again on his good leg. His eyes ran over her like a physical caress that left her quaking.

And just that easily, she didn't care about maintaining the upper hand. Couldn't even remember why it had seemed important.

She lifted her arms toward him and the bed dipped under his weight as he joined her. His hands slid around her back, rolling her toward him even as his mouth found hers again. "I don't want to crush you," he said against her lips.

"You won't." She pushed him even further until his shoulders were flat against the quilt, and she slid her leg across his hips until she was straddling him. She leaned over his chest, kissing his chin. His temple. His mouth. His hands were flexing against her waist, and she pulled them to her breasts.

He made a low sound in his throat that thrilled her to her core. The denim of his jeans felt rough beneath her, needlessly reminding her that there was so much more to come, and she slid away from him just enough to unfasten his straining fly.

And then, when she succeeded and for some unfathomable reason hesitated, he lifted an eyebrow and smiled faintly. "You gonna stop now?"

Her lips firmed. She'd helped him dress dozens and dozens of times by now.

She grasped the jeans and pulled them—as well as the boxers beneath—down his narrow hips, over cast and leg.

And then there was simply no amount of nurses' training or experience that could lessen the impact of Mason lying on her bed. For her.

Her heart pounded dizzily as her greedy gaze took him—all of him—in.

"Courtney."

"What?" She could barely form the simple word, and he gave that faint smile again.

"Take off your panties." His deep voice whispered over her nerve endings.

She moistened her lips, slipped the scanty bikini off her hips and stepped out of them.

He let out a long, audible breath. And then he held out his hand.

Shaking inside, she took it. He tugged and she mindlessly knelt on the mattress, then settled over him.

His hands caught her hips, pressing her harder against him, and a vague portion of her mind feared she'd actually begun purring. And then his hands slid up her spine, urging her torso toward him, and his mouth caught one breast, then the other.

She could have wept for the perfection in his touch. Almost of their own accord, her hips moved against his, maddening them both with the slide of her against him.

And then, despite his weighty, cumbersome cast, despite her own not inconsiderable height, he lifted her just enough to sink to the very depths of her.

She cried out and he went abruptly still. "Did I hurt you?"

Foolish tears were burning at the backs of her eyes. She shook her head, leaning against him to find his mouth. "No," she promised. She slowly rocked against him. He would never hurt her.

Not making love.

When he left, then she'd be hurt.

And even knowing that couldn't stop them now.

Not when he filled her so deeply, so completely. Not when she couldn't tell where his hard flesh stopped and her soft flesh began. And not when his hands tightened on her, urging himself deeper. And not when she felt him growing impossibly thicker, harder, and not when she felt herself flying into a million bits of ecstasy while he groaned her name and flew with her.

It was only later…much later…when she could draw normal breath again, when she could manage to unlock their fused hips and slip off of him, that they both recognized one important thing.

The condom was still sitting untouched on the nightstand.

Silently calling himself every vile name he could think of, Mason looked at the packet. He—ever prepared, ever safe—had forgotten the damn thing, even when it was sitting within arm's reach.

Courtney's long, curvaceously lithe body beside him suddenly moved. She pushed her hand through her tousled hair. Her amber gaze skittered over him, then away. "I suppose you think I did this deliberately."

"I wasn't thinking anything of the sort." His voice was flat with blame. Self-blame.

Her lovely throat worked. She scooted off the bed

and disappeared into her walk-in closet. When she came out, she had a thin black robe wrapped tightly around her that did nothing to help disguise the mind-boggling curves beneath. "Well, whatever you're thinking, you don't have to worry. It's totally the wrong time of month for me to conceive."

His jaw felt tight. "Wouldn't want anything to get in the way of 37892?" He rolled over to the side of the bed and managed to scoop up his boxers and work them on but not without some struggle. "Damn cast." He had two more weeks before they'd even entertain the idea of removing it, and he was going to be out of his tree by then.

She was chewing her lip. Her cheeks were pale. "Mason—"

He lifted his hand. "Don't. This is my fault. I knew better, and I still let myself get carried away."

Color suddenly filled her drawn face. "You think you're the only one responsible? Maybe it escaped your attention, Mason, but I started it."

He gave a bark of humorless laughter. "Believe me, honey. I noticed." He'd noticed so damn well that he hadn't thought of another single thing, least of all protecting her. Whether she wanted to be protected or not.

A pain set up residence between his eyes.

If he'd taken his chances with Connecticut and the doctors and the reporters there, all of this could have been avoided.

Courtney wouldn't have had the funds to invest in good ol' 37892 yet…and maybe she would have changed her mind with more time to think about it. She might have dated Dr. Feelgood on her own, and maybe she'd be looking at the whole white-picket-fence deal with him that she claimed she didn't want.

And they wouldn't have ended up burning the sheets again, only this time with the additional wrinkle of his failure to exercise even a semblance of caution.

"I don't care what the timing is," he said. "Good or bad. If you're pregnant, then—"

"I won't be," she interrupted emphatically. "So there's no point in even discuss—"

"Then I'll do what's right," he finished.

Her eyes widened. "And in your mind, that would be…what?"

"It won't involve me abandoning you. Pretending I'm not the father. No kid of mine will grow up not knowing where he comes from, the way I did."

"And that's all this theoretical child would be to you? A responsibility." It wasn't quite a question.

The nape of his neck felt itchy. "A child *is* a responsibility. That's what I've been telling you ever since I learned about your baby plan."

She pressed her lips together for a long moment. The high color faded from her face. The storm in her amber eyes calmed. "Well. I can assure you that your responsible nature won't be called into play," she said coolly. "The timing's wrong." The corners of her lips lifted, but there was no humor in her smile, either. "And that's something that I have been paying close attention to. Getting ready for number 37892, after all."

Then she turned and walked through the door to her bathroom, shutting it behind her.

She didn't come out.

Mason knew that she wouldn't. Not until she was sure he'd left her room.

He retrieved the crutches from the floor, as well as his jeans, which had fallen on top of them, and levered to his feet. At the bedroom doorway, he looked back.

The bathroom door was still closed. Her quilt-covered bed was tousled.

Something inside his chest ached, and he rubbed his hand against it.

Then, with a sigh, he left Courtney's bedroom and went into his own.

Plato stood in the hallway, looking in at him. Then the dog turned and padded into Courtney's room.

He didn't blame the dog.

If he didn't have to endure his own company, he wouldn't, either.

Chapter Eleven

"How's the leg coming?"

Mason sat on a chair on Courtney's back deck, watching Plato romp around in the snow that had fallen overnight.

She'd gone to church that morning. Probably to pray that their folly during the middle of the night wouldn't result in a pregnancy that would come with more complications than she wanted.

Namely...*him.*

"Mase?"

He focused on Cole's voice, coming from the cell phone he held to his ear. "Bad connection," he lied. "Leg's doing fine. Gonna be out of the cast in a few weeks." He wasn't going to entertain the notion that his leg wouldn't be ready, even if Courtney had cautioned that it might not be.

"Then you'll be ready to go back active after Thanksgiving," Cole was saying, and at the word *active,* Mason tuned in more carefully.

"Yeah. If not before." The cast was supposed to come off a few days before the holiday. "I could be back in Connecticut by then." He should have felt more enthusiasm at the prospect. His inactivity over the past weeks had driven him buggy. Not even going over some case files with Axel had been enough to alleviate that.

"No need to rush," Cole said. "I'll be in Wyoming for the holiday, anyway." Mason could hear a faint smile in his boss's voice. "My daughter-in-law invited me. Expect it'll drive Brody nuts, but driving him nuts is one of my remaining pleasures in life."

Mason still found it hard to believe that his boss had a son, even one he was estranged from more often than not.

But it just went to prove that—for men like them—families and work weren't a combination destined for success.

"We'll talk when I'm there," Cole finished. "And I can see for myself that you're not trying to get back before you're ready."

Mason's molars ground together. Yeah, he'd had a rocky start to his recovery. But since that first week here with Courtney, he'd been a model—okay, *nearly* model—patient.

At least he hadn't managed to crack his casts after that first episode.

The rest of the time, he'd alternated between grumpy and grumpier. It was still astonishing that she'd tolerated as much as she had.

"Fine," he told Cole. "Thanksgiving. But after that I'm back to work. Even if I have to ride a desk for a few days, I'm back to work."

Cole snorted. "Don't blow that smoke around, Mase. I know you've been meeting regularly with Ax."

He shifted in his chair. Plato was sniffing around the back edge of the property like he'd found something interesting. "All I did was work up a few profiles for some cases."

"And you haven't done any profiling since the bombing," Cole countered. "You had me put you in security, despite everything I said at the time. If I'd known all it would take to get you back to where your real talents lie was to break your arms and legs, I'd have done it years ago."

Mason politely told his boss what he could do with his comment. Cole responded with a rusty laugh before he hung up.

Mason shoved the phone in the pocket of the jacket that Axel had loaned him. It was too tight in the shoulders, but it was serviceable enough. He whistled to Plato, but the dog was still digging around in the corner of the yard, showing no signs of stopping.

He pushed to his feet and swung down the steps. He took the crutches only because he didn't want to have to put up with the stink of a wet cast on top of the inconvenience of the thing in the first place. "Plato, whatcha hunting, eh?" He reached the dog, and balancing on one crutch and holding his cast aloft over the snow, he leaned over and nudged the dog's big head aside.

A wet, bedraggled kitten was lying still in the snow.

Mason grimaced. "You had to find a dead kitten?"

Plato whined and pawed at the snow around the kitten. Afraid the dog would decide to use it as a toy, he leaned over and scooped it up in his hand.

The body was still warm. Still alive.

He found himself chuckling and realized his laugh sounded just as rusty as Cole's laughter had. He rubbed his thumb over the minuscule head, and the kitten's skinny, wet tail curled. The kitten couldn't have been more than a few weeks old. Mason tucked the little animal inside his shirt and looked at Plato. "Any more?"

But the dog had turned to face the house again. He wagged his tail and gave a soft bark.

"Good dog." Mason started for the house, and the dog trotted ahead of him. Inside, he shrugged out of his borrowed jacket and left the crutches propped against the table. He fished the kitten out from inside his shirt.

His eyes, or hers—Mason couldn't tell at this point— were open. He grabbed a clean dish towel and wrapped it around the cat. Then, even though he wasn't supposed to put weight on his cast, he limped over to the refrigerator without his crutches and poured a small amount of milk in a coffee mug.

With the cat in one hand and the milk in the other, he sat down at the kitchen table, where he'd earlier left the newspaper and his reading glasses. He slipped on the glasses and peered more closely at the cat, rubbing it with the towel until the short gray fur dried and stuck out at all angles and he could hear the faint rumble of a small purr. Then he dipped his finger in the milk and rubbed it over the kitten's tiny snout. "Come on, tiger," he murmured. "Show a little life so I've got a reason to find your mama." And the other kittens that had to be around, since he didn't think any cat could ever have just one kitten in a litter.

Watching silently from the back doorway, Courtney pressed her hand to her stomach. Plato lifted his head and noisily flopped his tail, apparently breaking Mason's intense concentration on the kitten, so small it was easily eclipsed by his big hand.

He looked up at Courtney over the rims of his narrow glasses, and her stomach took its usual free-falling tumble.

"I didn't hear you come in."

Spurred into motion by his voice, she finished closing the door behind her. "I figured." She unwound the plaid scarf she'd tossed around the shoulders of her coat and folded it over the back of the chair next to Mason.

Since she'd locked herself in her bathroom the night before—well, it had been the wee hours of the morning, really—she hadn't spoken two words to him.

Like the coward that she was, while he'd been in the bathroom, she'd left him only a written note telling him that she'd gone to church before she'd snuck out.

She'd heard the shower running, but since he hadn't left out the duct tape for her to see, she'd taken her cue that he wasn't interested in performing their usual shower ritual anymore.

Considering everything, she couldn't really blame him.

Now, she deliberately pushed aside the tangle of emotions inside her and finished pulling off her coat as she eyed Mason and the tiny kitten. "I'm doubting that you've been to a pet store at this hour on a Sunday morning. So, what gives?"

"Plato found him. Or her." His attention was firmly back on the little kitten as he coaxed it to lick another drop of milk off the tip of his finger. "Buried in the snow by the back fence."

Courtney looked through the window. There was a house under construction on the other side of the back fence, but it wasn't occupied. Her neighbors to the right had a cat, but she knew for a fact that she was at least twelve years old. Hardly a likely candidate for whelping a litter of kittens. And the couple that lived on the left had only two little dogs. "No sign of more kittens?"

He shook his head. "Didn't look. I went off Plato's lead."

"I doubt he'd lead you astray," she said. "And I'm glad to hear you weren't tramping around in the snow. I'll check in the corners of the garage after I change clothes." But it was hard to tear her eyes away from Mason.

She'd known he got along well with Plato. But then everyone did. Even self-proclaimed non-dog-lovers. But she hadn't given any thought to whether or not Mason was, in general, an animal person.

Despite the hours and days she'd spent in his company, living under the same roof, struggling not to get too sucked in to the alluring aura of domesticity, she realized yet again just how much she *didn't* know about him.

Unfortunately, when she witnessed something new—like now—it didn't do anything to lessen his appeal.

How could she ever imagine the sight of his big body, hunched over such a tiny little creature, would make something inside her ache in a way that had nothing to do with passion?

Her throat felt tight. She quickly escaped to her room to change out of the dress she'd worn to church and into a pair of jeans and a thick sweater. In the bathroom, she pulled her hair back in her usual ponytail and stared at herself in the mirror. "Nothing has changed," she told her reflection.

Unfortunately, the woman staring back at her with the pitying expression told her that everything had changed. It had been changing since the moment Mason had rolled into her house, and that slow, downhill slide had gone into free fall when he'd given her that incredibly beautiful baby rattle.

She truly believed that she couldn't possibly have conceived a child last night. She hadn't exaggerated. The timing was wrong.

"But you wish the timing was right," she whispered to her reflection. Not because she wanted a baby, period.

But because, from the moment she'd realized they'd both forgotten to use that darn condom, it had become startlingly clear that the baby she wanted was *his*.

Only his.

Nothing had changed. Mason was still going to leave.

And everything had changed.

The woman in her mirror gave her a sad smile, and she turned away.

He was still in the kitchen with the kitten. Only now, Plato had managed to perch his big, oversized body on a kitchen chair next to Mason and was resting his head on the table, his nose only inches away from the minuscule feline.

Afraid the burning behind her eyes would get out of control, she hurried past both the males in her household and went outside.

The cold was mercifully bracing as she tramped around the perimeter of her yard, pushing through the small drifts of snow for any sign of more kittens, even though she didn't expect to find any. Plato would have discovered them first, if there were any. So after her yard was bordered by her footprints, as well as Plato's, she gave up, went into the garage and used a flashlight to search out all the shadowy corners.

Again, no kittens. No mama cat.

The cold air was penetrating her sweater, and she

went back inside, rubbing her hands together as she nudged the door closed with her hip.

"Should have worn a coat," Mason said.

She shrugged. "When I was a kid, I used to run around in the wintertime wearing shorts. Drove my folks nuts." She peered around his shoulder at the kitten that was now curled into a ball, seemingly content in its bed of bright red kitchen towel. "We could take it to Evan. My cousin's husband? He's the vet around here."

"Dump it off on him?" Mason looked at her over the rim of his glasses, a frown on his face.

No." She shook her head. "I mean to have him— her—whatever it is—looked over."

"He can't have been in the snow for long," Mason said. "I don't think he would have survived."

Courtney couldn't disagree with that. She reached past Mason to run her finger gently over the sleeping kitten's fur. "Do you have pets?"

"I had a cat once." His expression closed, and he nudged Plato off the chair. "Never seen a dog that big sit on a chair like that."

"He knew lots of tricks already when I adopted him. A good friend of mine had raised him from a pup. When she died, I took him in."

He gave her a quick look. "What happened?"

"To Margaret, you mean?" She crossed her arms and leaned against the counter. "Pancreatic cancer." She looked at him. "She was one of my instructors from nursing school in Cheyenne. She was a foster mother, too. For the human variety, not just the canine. What happened to the cat you had?"

His brows yanked together. "My ex-wife took her."

The ex-wife again.

Courtney studied her thumbnail. "How long were you married?"

"What is this? Twenty questions again?"

"Just being inquisitive." She smiled coolly. "Do you still love her? Is that why you don't want to talk about it?"

He sighed noisily. "Do *you* like talking about your failures?"

He had a point. "Sorry." She nodded toward the kitten. "So, do you want Evan to look the kitten over?"

He grimaced. "Yeah. And no. I'm not still in love with Greta."

There should be no earthly reason for her to be relieved hearing it. But she was. Mostly because she knew Mason wasn't lying. If he didn't want to tell someone the truth, he simply didn't say anything at all.

That was something that she did know about him.

"Well, Sunday dinner is at my uncle Dan's today. You can bring the kitten. I'm sure Leandra and Evan will be there as usual."

"Dinner," he nearly barked. "I thought you meant taking the cat to his office or something. *You* can take the cat."

"You're the one who rescued it." She tilted her head slightly. "What is so horrifying to you about attending a simple dinner? You've been over to my folks'. What's so different about this?"

"It's Sunday dinner! That stuff's for family."

"That stuff is for whoever is welcomed," she corrected him mildly. "And when I saw my aunt and uncle at church this morning, they specifically mentioned they hoped you'd come."

His eyes narrowed slightly. "You mean they hope that

you go since you've been giving the whole Sunday deal a miss since I got here."

She shrugged. "Don't take it personally. Sunday afternoons are also when I have a chance to play catch-up around here. Laundry and housecleaning don't happen on their own. Everyone in my family is used to my hits and misses."

He didn't look entirely convinced. "Fine. Just so the cat can get looked over."

She hid a smile. "We'll need to leave in an hour or so."

He nodded grumpily and picked up the nearly empty mug he'd been finger-dipping from, and with one long arm, reached over to set it in the sink. Then he grabbed his crutches, pulled to his feet and headed out of the room.

But before he made it, he turned back around to scoop the kitten out of the towel and tuck it neatly inside his shirt pocket. "Body warmth," he muttered.

Then he crutched out of the kitchen.

Courtney looked down at Plato. The dog was staring after Mason, his dark brown eyes soft.

She rubbed his head between his ears. "I know," she murmured. "I love him, too."

Then she went through the arch to the dining room, stopping next to the computer on its narrow desk. She slowly sat down and moved the mouse.

The screen saver cleared.

Number 37892 came into view.

She stared at the computer screen for a moment. And then with the flick of a finger, she turned off the computer.

"She looks fine to me," Evan said later that afternoon after he'd gone to his truck to get the vet bag that went everywhere with him. He held up the kitten in his hand and tickled her little belly, which had grown round with all the milk she'd consumed. "A little too young to be weaned, but Mason's obviously got that covered."

He looked over at where Courtney and Mason were sitting, in the kitchen of her aunt and uncle's house, surrounded by several children who were all anxious to see the new kitten.

Everyone else who'd come to dinner was in the family room, loudly watching a football game. Loud, because half the room was rooting for one team and half for the other.

"It is strange that the mother cat wasn't nearby." Evan handed the kitten to Courtney. "She might have gotten trapped in a garage or something."

"I checked with both of my neighbors before we got here," she said. She cradled the cat so that Shelby and Chloe—the two oldest children—could stroke its fur. "Be gentle," she reminded them and looked back at Evan. "They haven't seen a stray cat around at all, either."

Evan sighed a little. "Well, if she doesn't turn up in the next day or so…" He shook his head, his gaze going to the children.

"Wouldn't there be other kittens?" Mason asked.

Evan lifted his shoulder. "Not necessarily, if the mother was particularly young herself. A first litter. Without being able to examine the cat, it's all speculation." He smiled and rose from the table, scooping up his three-year-old son, Lucas, as he did. The boy chortled and reached for the kitten, then smiled widely when the kitten snatched its tail out of his fingers. "Looks to me like you've got yourselves another family member," Evan commented. "Come on, Luke." He hefted his son up to his face. "Let's find your mom and Katie, and you can play with the kitties at home."

"Katie don't play," Lucas complained.

"Katie is one year old," Evan reminded him with a patient grin. "Soon enough, there will come a time when you'll wish you could get her to stop playing with you. I know, 'cause I had a little sister, too."

"Uh-huh," Lucas said emphatically. He peered over his father's shoulder as they left the kitchen, his little hand opening and closing in a wave.

"What are you gonna name her, Auntie Court?" Chloe and her soon-to-be cousin, Shelby, leaned shoulder to shoulder against the table.

"She's Mason's cat." Courtney ignored the sidelong look she earned from the man at that. "It's up to him."

"She's not my cat," he said.

"You found her."

"Plato found her. Guess that makes her Plato's."

The girls giggled wildly at that particular notion.

Courtney smiled, too, even though she knew that Mason wasn't entirely joking.

"Well." She handed the nameless kitten to him and rose. "I'm going to tell everyone goodbye so we can head out. Uncle Matt said he smells more snow coming, and I want to get home before it hits."

Mason had to either take the kitten or let her fall onto the table. The two little girls—one belonging to Ryan and one to Beck, the guy engaged to marry Lucy—had been stuck like glue to him and Courtney since they'd produced the kitten from the basket they'd brought her in.

"Plato can't name her," Shelby said seriously. "He's a *dog.*"

Chloe giggled. "He would only name her *woof.*"

"Woof the cat." Despite himself, Mason grinned. "Think I like it."

Chloe beamed at him. "Are you gonna marry Auntie Court?"

His grin suddenly felt strangled. "What?"

"No," Courtney said, sailing back into the kitchen. She swept her niece up in her arms from behind and kissed the back of Chloe's neck, making her laugh even harder, before setting her back on her feet. "Nobody is marrying Auntie Court." She treated Shelby to the same upswing and kiss. "Mr. Hyde's just a friend, remember?"

Chloe wrinkled her nose and eyed Mason. She touched his cast with gingerly fingertips. "Does your leg hurt?"

"Not anymore."

"Does your face hurt?" Shelby stared up at him, innocence personified.

He saw the way Courtney caught her lip in her teeth as her startled gaze turned toward him. "Not anymore."

"How'd you get it hurt?"

The kitten was curled on his arm, purring. He could feel its faint vibration, even though it was too soft to hear. "My leg or my face?"

"Your face," Shelby replied immediately. "Lucy already told me you got your leg broke from a truck. You're not supposed to get in front of trucks that are moving."

"You're right about that," he agreed ruefully.

Courtney reached for his crutches, propped out of the way near the door, and held them out to him. "We should get going."

Strangely enough, he ignored the bailout.

Shelby was still watching him curiously. There was

no fear in her face. No horror. Just a child's simple curiosity.

"I got hit with a lot of broken glass," he told her with huge understatement. "It was a long time ago in another accident."

Chloe's face crunched up even more. "My dad broke a glass in our kitchen and he got a piece stuck in his toe. He was *mad,*" she added. "But my mom picked it out and put a bandage on it. You must have had a *lot* of bandages."

He nodded. "Yup. I did."

Evidently satisfied, Shelby touched his cast. "Can we sign your cast? Jenny Tanner's brother at school had a cast on his arm, and everyone in his class signed their name on it."

Chloe nodded. "But you don't have any on yours. Can we?"

"Girls—" Courtney started.

"You'd have to find a pen." Mason cut her off. Her amber eyes widened a little. Then they turned all soft and dangerous again, and he wished he would have just taken the crutches and bailed like she'd obviously expected.

The girls ran out of the kitchen.

"Glass?" Courtney asked.

"And metal and whatever else was part of the building that exploded," he said in a low tone that wouldn't carry.

She held the crutches against her. "What happened?"

"I didn't stop a psychotic bomber quick enough. He liked targeting Canadian day care centers."

She looked horrified. "Did you catch him?"

"Once I'd gotten all of the kids and staff out of the building. Yeah." He waited a beat. "I killed him before the bomb blew." He'd known he hadn't enough time left to get out of the building after making sure everyone else was away, but he'd been damn certain that the other guy wouldn't, either.

Her lips pressed together. "I think I'm glad," she said after a moment.

"It was just a job."

The corners of her lips turned upward. "Right."

The girls came running back into the kitchen, both bearing black markers. And then they were bent over his cast for long enough that he stopped wondering what Courtney was really thinking to worry about just what the little girls *were* writing.

Turned out that six- and seven-year-old girls didn't just sign their names. They had to draw flowers and hearts around them, too.

"Thanks," he said when they were finally finished.

Courtney wasn't even trying to hide her smile.

"You sign it, too," Chloe demanded, holding the pen up to her.

Without looking at him, Courtney leaned over the cast, near his ankle, and wrote. He tried to see what it said, but the angle was impossible.

By then, Mallory had come into the kitchen. And she, too, needed to sign the cast.

And then Mason found himself sitting there while everyone in the whole damn house signed the cast.

By the time they were done, and he and Courtney were finally making an escape—and it *did* feel like an escape—there was writing over ninety percent of the thing, and Courtney was smiling like the cat who'd stolen the cream.

She waited while he pulled himself into her backseat, as usual with his leg stretched across the seat, then handed him his crutches as well as the basket containing Woof. "That wasn't so terrible, was it?"

He eyed the doodles and the names and the comments that littered his cast. "I thought you planned to get home before the snow started," he said.

Her smile didn't dim. She looked up at the sky, where snowflakes had begun drifting down. "Oh, well. Plans change. We'll get home, anyway." Then she closed the car door and went around to the driver's side.

Mason looked down at the kitten he held.

If he could have, he'd have blamed the hollow ache inside him on cat claws.

But the kitten just lay there curled against his chest, silently purring.

Chapter Twelve

"So you're positive?" Mason eyed Courtney's face closely.

If she lied, he'd know it. He'd see it in her eyes.

"Yes," she assured. "I'm positively *not* pregnant." It was six days since the night they'd made love. She set the plate containing a meat loaf sandwich in front of him and turned back to the sink. "I told you the timing was wrong, and turns out, I was right."

He eyed her back. She was wearing a long-sleeved black running top and matching body-skimming running pants. Her hair was tied back in a ponytail, and she had a red winter scarf wrapped around her neck.

He could see that she was telling the truth.

But he couldn't tell if she was relieved or not.

"Then nothing can get in the way of number 37892 anymore," he said.

"Right." Her voice was chipper. She dried her hands

on a towel and picked up the gloves that she'd left sitting on the counter. "I'll be back in plenty of time to drive you to the hospital. Do you need anything else before I go?"

He needed plenty.

But he wasn't going to ask and she knew it.

He shook his head. "Thanks for the sandwich."

She just smiled and headed for the door, stopping only long enough to pet Plato where he was lying by the door, his big body curled protectively around tiny little Woof.

And then she was pulling on the gloves and slipping out the back door. Through the window, Mason could see her begin the routine of stretches she religiously performed before she went on her runs. Didn't matter that there was still a thin layer of snow on the ground or that the air was cold enough to send rings around her head when she breathed.

His appetite gone, Mason pushed aside the plate and limped into the dining room. He was having his leg x-rayed that afternoon to see if his cast would be coming off the following week as scheduled or if he would only be graduating to a smaller, more walking-friendly cast.

Either way, there would be no more reason for him to stay with Courtney. He could head back to his anemic apartment and get back to work.

That fact should have filled him with relief.

He made a face, sat down at her computer and turned it on, then sent an email to Cole using a convoluted path of servers.

And then he just sat there in front of the computer, looking at nothing in particular.

He needed to remember that he and Courtney had dodged a bullet.

No baby.

Not one of his, at any rate.

Courtney would be gone for at least an hour on her run, so he pushed away from the computer desk and half jumped, half limped down the hall to his bedroom. He'd already read all of the books he'd brought with him. And he'd read all of the ones on Courtney's bookshelf that he didn't already have.

Turned out they had similar tastes.

He looked around the bedroom, trying to envision it as a baby's nursery.

The vision came much too quickly, and he blamed it on the fact that he'd seen Courtney's choices for furniture and such on the damn computer.

When his cell phone rang, he nearly jumped out of his skin. Shaking his head at himself, he pulled it out of his pocket. "Hyde."

"Clay," Axel said with laughter in his voice. "You busy?"

Making himself crazy? Definitely. "Not at the moment."

"Courtney out?"

His eyes narrowed. "Why do I have the feeling that you already know?"

"Because we just saw her running past us. Be there in a sec." The line went dead.

Mason exhaled and headed out to the living room just in time to see Axel's truck pulling into the driveway.

The "we" part was quickly explained when he saw Tristan Clay, Axel's uncle, climb out of the truck, too.

Mason sat down in one of the chairs and waited. As he'd expected, Axel didn't stand on ceremony. He just walked right on in. "Hey."

Mason looked from the younger man to the older. "What's going on?"

Tristan smiled faintly and held up the thin file folder that he was carrying. "Axel showed me these profiles you've worked up."

Mason eyed Axel. "Helped work up," he corrected. "And you've got a big mouth." Cole had known about Mason's help pulling together a few profiles on some cases Axel had on his plate. And now Tristan did, too.

"I want you to come and work for me," Tristan said.

Mason raised his brows. "I already work for HW."

Tristan nodded once. "On Cole's side of the operation. All international." He sat on the arm of the couch and tapped the file against his thigh. "We've got needs on the domestic side, too. One in particular that I believe you can fill."

"Cole know you're poaching on his side of the fence?"

The other man smiled, looking unperturbed. "I'm not worried about Cole."

Neither was Mason when it came right down to it. "I got out of profiling a long time ago."

"After the Canadian day care incident." Tristan nodded. "I know."

Mason figured that Tristan probably knew what had followed, as well, since he was as close to being the number two man in the agency as it was possible to get. What he didn't know was how much his nephew Axel knew about his past.

Despite working together on numerous cases, Mason had never discussed it with him.

"But these—" Tristan tapped the file folder again "—clearly prove that you haven't lost the gift. There has already been some action on two of the cases where the feds were previously stuck against a brick wall." He smiled faintly. "'Course, you'd be working mostly out of Weaver, which—as you've probably discovered— doesn't offer quite the conveniences as Cole's shop does."

Mason was shaking his head before Tristan even stopped talking. "No. I'm not moving to Weaver."

"You'd be well compensated."

It wasn't the money. He was already well compensated for the work he did. If he wanted to, he could retire right now. "Thanks, but no thanks."

"Stubborn. Cole warned me."

Mason almost smiled. "I appreciate the offer. But Weaver's not for me."

"Too bad." Tristan slanted a look at his nephew, then pushed to his feet and went to the door. "I think you'd be a good addition around here. If you change your mind, let me know. I can always put a guy like you to good use." He pulled open the door and stepped outside.

Axel followed him. "Just give it some time to roll around in your head," he advised, hanging back. "No harm. No foul."

"I can't stay here."

"Because of Court?"

Mason grimaced. "What makes you think that?"

Axel gave him a look. "This is Weaver, man. You were kissing in public. Unless you like having water-balloon fights with condoms or something, you're obviously sleeping with her. And besides all that, anyone with decent vision—and mine is perfectly fine—can see the sparks flying in the air when you're with each other."

Mason muttered an oath. He shoved out of the chair and started to pace, but there wasn't a lot of satisfaction in it when he had to hop on one foot to do it. "Nothing's private in this town." Except the fact that they hadn't used a condom at all. Except the fact that he hadn't gotten her pregnant, anyway.

He knew for certain that Courtney wouldn't have shared those details with anyone. And he sure as hell hadn't.

"There are a few things a person can keep a lid on if they try." Axel shrugged. "Tara's pregnant again, and we've managed to keep it quiet for the past month and a half."

Mason stared.

"We wanted to wait until she was further along before we shared it. She had a miscarriage a while back that only we and her OB know about, too."

"She's okay?"

Axel nodded. "Perfect. And as of this week, she's a solid four months along, with no indication that anything'll go wrong."

Mason shoved his hand through his hair. "How do you do it?" Yeah, Axel was younger than he was. He hadn't been with the agency as long. But he'd still seen his share of action. He knew how things could turn bad in the blink of an eye. "Act like you've got a normal life?"

"Because it *is* a normal life," Axel returned.

"Tara knows what you really do." She had to, since Axel had been assigned to protect her when her twin brother, Sloan, had come to the agency for help. "She knows you don't—" he air-quoted "—breed horses."

"I do—" Axel air-quoted "—breed horses. Real horses. But she knows I also work for Tris. It's normal for us, because we make it that way. Because being together is what is important."

"And if you don't come walking in the door some

weekday afternoon at five o'clock because you ended up on the wrong side of a weapon, that's gonna be normal?" Mason shook his head. "I don't believe it."

"Cops get married," Axel returned. "Anyone who's a first responder gets married. They have lives."

"And a damn high divorce rate," he muttered. And statistically speaking, he knew the success of marriages for HW operatives was even rarer.

"Anyone who gets married takes that chance." Axel glanced out the doorway. "Just because Greta couldn't take it doesn't mean Courtney can't."

Mason stiffened. "Who the hell said anything about *that?*"

Axel just shook his head. "Dude. You have got it bad."

"She's too young, anyway. I've got thirteen years on her, for God's sake."

At that, Axel laughed. "Twenty-six years on earth, a hundred and six years in her soul. Tara said something like that once about her. Called her an old soul. Said it's one of the things that makes her such a good nurse. That ability she's got to let people just be who they are. If you haven't noticed that about her by now—" he shook his head "—then maybe I do need my vision checked. As far as I'm concerned, age differences—one way or the other—only become an issue if you make them one."

"She's your cousin. I'd think you'd want to protect her a little more."

"From the likes of you?" Axel rolled his eyes and walked toward the door. "That is one of the most asinine things I've ever heard come out of your mouth." He lifted his hand. "Think about Tristan's offer. Profiling instead of direct security? Would get you out of the way of flying objects more often. It's not quite a banker's nine-to-five, but in our business it's as close as you're ever likely to get."

Mason didn't reply.

He watched Axel stride to his truck, where his uncle was waiting, and drive away.

He slowly pushed the door closed.

Plato and his new sidekick had padded into the living room. Even as Mason watched, the dog picked the kitten up in his mouth and set her on the couch. Then he jumped up beside her, circled a few times and settled down with a harrumphing sigh.

"Talk about the odd couple."

Plato just wagged his tail a few times. If the dog understood, or agreed, it was pretty obvious that he didn't care.

"Healing nicely." Dr. Jackman was peering at the computerized X-ray of Mason's leg. He tapped the end of his pen against the screen. "There. And there." He tapped again. "And there. Those are the sites of the fractures." He tapped once again. "That's where the first pin became infected." He nodded and slid his pen into his lapel pocket as he turned to face Mason. They were sitting in his office at the hospital. "It all looks good." The gray-haired doctor smiled at Courtney. "Nice job, Nurse Clay."

Courtney shook off the praise. "All I did was give him a few meals and make sure he took his meds on time."

She'd done a helluva lot more, Mason figured, but that was none of the orthopedist's business. "Good enough to cut me out of this thing early?"

Courtney suddenly pushed out of her chair. Mason eyed her. She didn't look at him, though. Her eyes were trained solely on the doctor.

"Actually—" Dr. Jackman considered for a moment "—yes. You'll need to follow up with a few weeks of physical therapy to strengthen the muscles again. But yes."

The answer took a moment to sink in. Then Mason leaned forward in his chair. "Seriously." He knocked on the cast. "You're gonna let me out of this place without the fiberglass monster."

Dr. Jackman nodded. "I'll call down and arrange it with my technician."

"I can," Courtney offered abruptly. "I saw Rodney down in Emergency when we got here."

The doctor nodded. He scribbled on Mason's medical chart and handed it to her, then stuck out his hand. "Congratulations, Mr. Hyde. Try to avoid getting in front of moving vehicles for a while."

Mason shook the man's hand, then pushed to his feet. "I will." He grabbed his crutches and followed Courtney out into the corridor.

"Congratulations, indeed," she told him with a whisper of a smile. "In a few more minutes, you'll be a free man again." She walked briskly along the tile corridor. She was already wearing her nurse's getup. The blue scrubs were as unfitted and loose as her running gear had been formfitting, and he found her just as mesmerizing either way. "Now you have something else to celebrate."

Else?

He caught her by the back of her shirt, halting her midstep. "I'm not celebrating the fact that you're not pregnant," he said.

"Shh!" She looked around them. "Keep your voice down, would you please?"

"I will when you stop spouting bologna like that."

She jerked her shoulders, and her shirt slid out of his grasp. "Don't pretend that you're sorry about it." She took off again along the wide hallway.

The hospital wasn't particularly huge.

But Mason knew if he didn't keep up with her, he'd still end up in a maze, because there wasn't a hospital he'd ever been in that hadn't been constructed that way. Not in the United States or elsewhere.

He followed, moving fast on the crutches until he caught up to her. "You're the one who should be celebrating," he said in a low voice. "Now you can have your baby with no complications to mess it up. Your plan can proceed just the way you want it to."

She whirled on her rubber-soled heel so fast he nearly ran into her. "The only thing about any of this that has gone as planned is *you*. You've healed well." She lifted her hand and smiled humorlessly. "So, voilà. Now you can get back to your life. I know that's the only thing that you want." She turned again and strode away, soon turning a corner and disappearing from view.

He hurried after her, his crutches thumping the tile. He caught up with her just as she reached the emergency department.

Which was, for the first time in his experience, full of people. All of the beds were curtained off, and people in scrubs and lab coats were moving quickly around.

Courtney didn't look as surprised as he felt, though. She just continued out into the waiting room, holding open one side of the swinging doors for him. "You'll have to wait out there." She nodded toward the molded plastic chairs. Most of them, too, were full. "I'll see how quickly Rodney can get to you."

He wanted to stop. To tell her…something. But what? Their business was all but complete. She'd made it plain that she was organizing her life exactly the way she'd wanted, and he could get back even earlier than he'd hoped to what he knew.

Work.

His crutches cleared the doorway, and she stepped back, letting the door swing closed.

It nearly hit him on the butt.

Wyatt—the only guy he'd seen her dance with at the Halloween thing other than her brother—was sitting at the reception desk, giving him a sympathetic look.

Mason ignored it and aimed for one of the chairs—the only one that wasn't surrounded by sneezing kids. He sat down and rested the crutches on the empty chair beside him.

He stared at his cast, stretched out in front of him. The black writing all over the blue surface seemed to leap out at him. His finger traced one of the hearts that little Chloe had drawn. He angled his head, but he still couldn't read what Courtney had written around his ankle.

"Looks like you have a lot of family and friends." The old man across from him was looking at Mason's cast, too.

"I don't have any family," Mason returned, hoping the guy would go back to his wheezing and keep his comments to himself. He folded his arms over his chest and closed his eyes.

"Then you got a lot of friends." Obviously, his hint hadn't been received.

Mason sighed. He opened his eyes. "What're you here for?"

"Emphysema," the guy wheezed. "Lifelong smoker." He patted the narrow oxygen tank that was sitting in a wheeled contraption next to him. "Now this is my lifelong friend."

At that moment, Mason was glad he'd never taken up the habit of cigarettes.

"You're not from around here," the guy continued. He was nodding his bald head. "Can't breathe for nothing anymore, but the memory's still good."

"Connecticut," he said.

The guy's thin eyebrows rose. "You're the one staying with the Clay girl, then."

He wasn't even surprised anymore at the well-developed grapevine that Weaver seemed to possess. "Guess I am."

"Heard you're a real live hero."

Mason grimaced. He'd never particularly felt like one. He'd just tried to do what was right. Live up to what he'd been paid to do.

He wasn't getting paid a thing here in Weaver. Not with Courtney. And he damn sure wasn't feeling heroic when it came to her.

He eyed the old man. "Anybody here with you?"

The man coughed into his plaid handkerchief and shook his head. "Ain't got no one. Never seemed to find the time." He coughed some more, then took a drag on his oxygen line. Judging by the attachment at the end, Mason figured he was supposed to have it leading into his nose all the time and not hanging around his neck like some necklace. "Live over in Braden, but gotta come here to Weaver for the fancy doctors."

"Mason?" He looked up when he heard Courtney's voice. She was standing at the double doors again. "You can come on back."

He grabbed his crutches—for the last time, he figured—and stood. He stuck his hand out to the old guy. "Good luck."

The man's lips stretched into a smile. His hand trembled, but his handshake was still firm. "G'luck to you, too, young man." His gaze slanted toward Courtney. "She's a catch. The kind to make time for."

"That she is." He was glad, though, that she was standing far enough away that she was unable to hear them. He swung around on the crutches and headed toward Courtney.

She didn't meet his gaze as she waited for him to pass through. She pointed. "The last bed on the right."

Mason held back. "That guy with the emphysema out there needs attention more than I do."

Her amber gaze slid to him, then away again. "Different issues," she said. "Mr. Martin will be seen as soon as one of the doctors is available. You've already seen Dr. Jackman. Now all you need is for Rodney to remove your cast." She held out her hand toward the far bed. "And clear the exam area again as quickly as possible," she added pointedly.

He headed toward the last bed. She followed him and set his medical chart on the stainless steel counter, then gave the curtain a tug. It swung smoothly into place. "Rodney will be with you in a few minutes."

"Wait a minute. Where are you going?"

She still didn't look at him. "They're so slammed, they asked me to clock in early."

"*They?* Or are you just looking for an excuse to get away from me?" Not that he had any reason to blame her for that.

Her lips twisted a little. "I'm just trying to do my job," she said. "Of all people, you should understand that. Don't worry, though. I talked to Ax. He'll come and get you when you're finished. He said just give him a call when you're done." She ducked out from behind the curtain.

He sat on the edge of the examining table and stared down at his cast. After two months of it, he wanted the thing off so badly he could taste it.

There was also a part of him that wished it had to stay in place.

Because then *he* could have a reason to stay, too.

Courtney managed a friendly smile as she coaxed a feverish little Bethany Jones onto the exam table two beds down from Mason. She could hear the distinctive pitch of the saw that Rodney was using to cut off Mason's cast.

Inside, it felt like *she* was being cut in two.

"What's that noise?" Bethany gave her mom a worried look.

"Someone's getting a cast taken off," Courtney soothed. "Nothing to worry about."

Bethany's mother sat on the table beside her daughter. "Remember when Daddy had a cast on his arm? That's what it sounded like when he got it off, too." She smoothed her daughter's hair back from her face and looked at Courtney. "Will the doctor be very long?"

"Not long." She knew that the on-call doctor had been called in to help with the unexpected load. She took Bethany's vitals and noted in the chart all the information the doctor would need, then tucked the chart in its holder and excused herself.

The sound of the saw stopped.

Which meant Mason's cast was now a thing of the past.

Which meant that his time in Weaver was a thing of the past, too.

She swallowed the knot in her throat. What she wanted to do was find a private room somewhere and cry her heart out.

Instead, she forced herself to wash her hands and did what she was trained to do.

She moved on to the next patient.

It took four hours for the waiting room to get cleared. By then, the time for Courtney's usual shift had already begun. She worked straight through until morning and tried to tell herself that she wasn't really waiting for Mason to try to call her. To talk to her.

Just as she'd arranged, her cousin had driven him home when he'd finished with the cast removal. If Mason hadn't gotten a clue by now, it was because he didn't want to. So really, what was there left to talk about?

She wasn't going to beg the man to stay with her, when he was clearly anxious to leave.

It was snowing lightly when she drove home from the hospital, and the tension inside her had relaxed a little by the time she got there.

The porch light was on. And beyond the plantation shutters in the front window, she could see a warm glow.

As usual, Mason had left the light on for her.

He hadn't left, after all.

She parked in the driveway and nearly ran into the house. Plato and Woof were sleeping on the floor by the door. Her dog lifted his head and stood. He pushed his head into her hand even before she had a chance to set down her car keys and purse.

Her heart sank all over again.

"He's gone, isn't he?"

Plato just stood by her side. His tail didn't wag.

She sucked her lip between her teeth and made herself

walk through the house. When she reached Mason's bedroom, she could only stand in the doorway.

His bed was made with military precision. The stacks of books were gone from the nightstand.

The only thing out of place was an envelope sitting on the dresser.

A part of her—the part that ached because he could so easily walk away—wanted to rip it in two.

She inhaled deeply and pulled out the contents.

Just two items. A folded piece of paper surrounding a check. She barely glanced at the check. He was just paying the last of the agreed-upon room and board. She looked at the paper, though.

"Raising a family gets expensive," he'd written. "What with a child and a dog and a cat."

Her chest tightened and her knees felt shaky.

She sank down on the foot of his bed, glanced at the check he'd made payable to her and went stock-still.

The exorbitant amount jumped out at her. She could have opened an entire orphanage with the amount he'd written.

Her fingers closed jerkily around the check. "Oh, Mason." How could he try to give her this when all she wanted was him?

Plato padded into the room, carrying Woof in his gentle jaws. He smoothly leapt up onto the mattress beside her and deposited the kitten in her lap.

Courtney lowered her head over them both and cried.

Chapter Thirteen

"I'm sorry, sir, but you can't take that on the plane with you."

Mason gritted his teeth.

It had taken him all night just to get from Weaver to the airport in Cheyenne. Now if he could only get *on* the damn plane.

He eyed the security agent and held up the thick, black plastic bag that contained his cast. It was cut into several separate pieces, but they were still bulky. "It's a fiberglass cast," he said for about the hundredth time. "Run it through your machines or whatever you need to do, but it's going on the plane with me. I'm not having it crushed in a pile of luggage." He wished to hell that he'd just waited long enough to arrange a private flight through HW. But no, he'd been in too much of a damn hurry to get away from Weaver.

"I'm sorry," the kid was saying. His gaze was glued

to Mason's face, and his Adam's apple bobbled in his throat as if he was afraid that Mason was going to resort to violence.

He wasn't. He just wanted—needed—to get on the plane and get home so he could get back to work. Get back to what he was good at.

There'd be no Plato. No Woof.

No Courtney.

He'd left the cat behind, because it was the sensible thing to do. He couldn't take care of a kitten, even though it would grow into an independent cat. For that matter, he couldn't take care of a cat.

Not with his lifestyle.

He realized the kid was eyeing him with increasing alarm. The last thing Mason wanted was to get hauled into the security office because he looked like a suspicious traveler. "Fine." He grabbed his duffel bag off the conveyor belt, and with the unwieldy bag in his other hand, he moved out of the security line.

He could feel anxious eyes boring into his back as he made his way back through the airport.

It still felt strange walking with two shoes and no cast after two months, and as much as he hated to admit it, his leg was aching and tired. He could have sat in any number of chairs that he passed, but he was well aware that two uniformed officers were following him at a not-very-discreet distance.

Being irritated with them didn't accomplish anything. They were just trying to do their job the best they could, too, and he wasn't exactly the picture of a harmless tourist. Not with his face. Not with his jeans that had one leg split up to the thigh. And definitely not with the bulky bag he refused to surrender.

He finally exited the terminal and climbed into the

first taxi that came available. He asked for the closest hotel, then leaned his head back against the seat and sighed. He'd regroup and arrange a charter, once and for all.

"Going home for the holiday?" the taxi driver asked.

"Something like that." It took no effort at all to imagine the get-together that the Clays would put on for Thanksgiving. It would be crowded and noisy, full of opinions and laughter and chasing children and crying babies.

He pinched his eyes closed. Courtney had been home from the hospital for several hours.

She'd seen the check he'd left.

He rubbed his hand against the hollow in his chest and looked down at the garbage bag beside him.

He still didn't know what stupid sentimentality had made him keep the thing. Just because it had been scribbled on by a bunch of people? But when Rodney had started to pitch the pieces he'd cut away into the trash, Mason had stopped him. And instead, the technician had dropped them in the black bag. When he was finished, he'd tied the top closed and handed it to Mason. "Sentimental value, eh?"

Mason had just taken the bag and, wearing a paper bootie on his bare foot, he'd left the hospital before he could find Courtney and tell her to hell with plans....

And once he'd started moving, he hadn't let himself stop. He'd tied up his loose ends at the house, threw the ball for Plato a few times and let Woof claw her way all around his shoulders. And when midnight struck with no word from Courtney, he'd called the only cab in town and paid him a fortune to drive him to Cheyenne.

If he had just pitched the bag in the trash at airport security, he could have been on his way back to

Connecticut, once and for all. And from there, it would have been a quick matter to get Cole to assign him to a security detail—anything, even if it meant piggybacking on someone else's case—as long as it was out of the U.S. of A., the country of Courtney Clay.

The cab pulled up in front of the airport hotel. "Need help with your stuff?"

Mason's lips twisted. "I got it." He paid the fare, added a tip and climbed out.

In minutes, he was inside a bland, sterile hotel room.

He dropped his stuff on the bed and moved across to the window, pulling open the drapes to display the grand view of a crowded parking lot. The sight of a woman with long blond hair crossing between the cars jolted him.

But after that first glance, he looked away. Not Courtney.

She wouldn't know he was in Cheyenne for one thing. And for another, even if she did, she wouldn't follow him. Why would she?

He turned on the television to drown out the sound of his own thoughts and flipped open the refrigerated minibar to find something to drown out the rest.

He extracted a beer. "It's five o'clock somewhere," he muttered and popped it open, then threw himself down on the hard mattress. He set the beer aside and dragged the bag close enough to untie it.

He hadn't looked inside it after Rodney had dropped the pieces in the bag. Now, he slowly pulled the fiberglass pieces out, fitting them together like a puzzle.

He wanted the part that had been around his ankle.

The part that Courtney had signed that he hadn't been able to read, not even when he'd tried using a hand mirror one night when she'd been at work.

The part, he realized after he'd pulled all of the pieces out of the bag, that Rodney had cut neatly in half.

Sighing, he tried to ignore the shaking of his hands as he fit the two pieces together.

And then all he could do was stare at the sawed edges of her writing.

"Even the best plans can change," she'd written, "when you find something better than 37892."

He closed his eyes as pain—worse than anything he'd ever felt—ripped through him. Pain of his own making because he was too damn stubborn to see what had been in front of him all along.

And then, doing the smartest thing he'd done in the past twelve hours, he pulled out his phone and he called Cole.

Courtney saw the truck as soon as she rounded the corner on her street. It was parked directly in front of her house.

She had a stitch in her side from running too hard and too fast for too long. But no amount of running had been able to get the pain out of her chest.

Shaking her head at her own foolishness, she pressed a hand to her side and slowed to a walk as she finished crossing the distance to her house.

She gave the truck—a delivery truck, she realized as she got closer—another glance as she passed it. One of her neighbors must have purchased some building supplies from one of the big-box places in Gillette. Two men were unloading a shrink-wrapped pallet onto the sidewalk, and they gave her a nod. "Afternoon."

"Afternoon." She turned up the walkway, which she'd shoveled clean of snow that morning when she couldn't sleep, and wondered how long it would be before she would be able to sleep again.

She supposed that depended on how long it took a broken heart to heal.

She pulled off her gloves and went up the front steps, trying hard not to look at the wooden ramp that was still in place.

She'd call Ryan before she went to work and ask him to pull it off. The one over the back steps, too. The sooner she got rid of the evidence that Mason had been there, the sooner she could start pretending she could forget him.

She walked in through the front door and stopped dead in her tracks.

Mason was sitting at her computer desk, Plato and Woof lying by his feet. "You ran longer than I expected," he greeted.

She actually felt dizzy.

"What are you doing here?" Her voice sounded breathless, and her pride hoped he'd attribute it to her running.

Her heart, though, didn't care about anything except the sight of him. He was clean shaven and he'd had a haircut. The thick hair that had grown unruly and over-long was now short and brushed away from his hard-hewn face. He was wearing a white button-down shirt tucked into black jeans. Jeans that hadn't been cut up to accommodate a cast. "You, uh, you left," she reminded him needlessly.

"Yeah. You going to close the door, or do you plan on kicking me out of it?"

She realized that the door was still open behind her, and she pushed it closed against the cold air. "That depends on whether you deserve to be kicked out."

His brows pulled together in a frown. "It's not about what I deserve."

She crossed her arms tightly, hoping to hold in her shaking. "Mason, what are you doing here?"

He glanced at her computer. "It was off," he murmured. "I noticed it before but didn't take note of it until it was too late."

"So?" She lifted her chin a notch. "Turning it off saves electricity."

"You quit looking at the cryobank's website," he said. "The last time you looked at it was the day Plato found Woof."

It was better that her hackles rose, because she could concentrate on them, rather than the aching inside her. "More spying?"

He didn't deny it. "Why?

She swallowed the knot in her throat and looked at him, not answering.

"What did you find that's better than 37892?" His pale green eyes stared back at her. "I finally read what you wrote on my cast."

"It's not like it was a secret," she reminded him. "It's been there for the past week!"

"Yeah, well, for the past week, I couldn't *see* behind my ankle, which is pretty much where you wrote it."

"Don't act irritated with me," she retorted. "If you wanted to know what it said, you could have asked anyone. Even me."

His lips thinned. "I didn't come here to argue about things that don't even matter."

She took an involuntary step forward. "Then what *are* you here for?"

"For you." His answer was quiet. Simple.

And it stopped her in her tracks.

She trembled harder than ever, afraid to let herself believe he could possibly mean what her heart was begging him to say. "Why? Because you feel badly now that you know I've changed my mind about using the cryobank? You can have your check back, by the way." She gestured with one arm, only to quickly rewrap it around herself. "It's in that envelope on the table. I was going to mail it back to you this afternoon."

"If I hadn't wanted you to have it, I wouldn't have left it."

She forced her chin up. "And as you now realize, I don't *need* it. I can support myself," she reminded him, less tartly than she would have preferred. "I can even afford to take care of Plato and Woof—" she waved her hand toward the two animals, who were watching their exchange "—since you abandoned her, too."

His lips tightened. "Would you rather have had me take her back to an apartment that I'm never at? Break Plato's heart?" He shook his head and clawed his fingers through his hair. "This is not going how I planned."

"Well." Her jaws felt clenched together. "Plans change, don't they?"

Her blood pounded heavily inside her head when he started crossing the room toward her. He didn't stop until he was only a few feet away. "What'd you find that's better than 37892?"

His eyes were searching hers, seeming to look straight through to her soul. And the only thing she had left was the truth. "Not what." Her voice sounded raw. *"Who."*

His scar was standing out whitely. "You want my baby."

She blinked hard, but the tears burning behind her eyes wouldn't go away. "I want everything," she whispered. "You. Our baby. The whole deal. But the only thing I *need* is you."

"You can do better than me." His voice turned husky.

She shook her head. "No. I really don't think so." She swiped a tear from her cheek. Took a bracing breath. "But I don't want you here unless this is where *you* want to be. I don't need you throwing yourself in front of this particular bus to save me from being hurt, Mason. I can take most anything but that."

He closed his eyes for a long moment. When he opened them again, they were bloodshot. And damp. "Then save me."

She pressed her hands to her chest. "Oh, Mason."

"There aren't many things I've loved in my life," he said gruffly. "And everything that I had, I've lost. It's always been safer not to let myself feel anything. And then I met you. Doling out kisses for five bucks a pop. I don't want to end up like that guy at the hospital, old and alone because he didn't stop to make time for what mattered. *You* are what matters, Courtney. If I'm not too late."

She couldn't bear another moment.

She reached out and wrapped her arms around him, stretching her cheek up toward his. "You haven't lost me."

His arms came around her, nearly lifting her off her feet. "Not yet."

"Not ever," she vowed. She pulled back to look into his eyes. "That's the thing about us Clays." She smiled shakily. "We're stubborn. And when we find what we want, we don't budge."

He lowered his forehead to hers. She could feel the charge of his heart against hers. "It might take some stubbornness. I'm told I'm thickheaded."

She gave a tearful laugh. "Well, you are. And I love you anyway."

His arms tightened around her. "I'm thirteen years older than you," he reminded her. "I'm not getting any younger. And my job isn't going to go away. I'll do what I can to stay in Weaver. Tristan's got some ideas about that—"

She caught his face in her hands. "See? Thickheaded. I love you, Mason. Just as you are. I couldn't care less how old—"

He covered her mouth with his. And when the words died on her lips and her knees had gone to gelatin, he let her up for air. "I'm not getting any younger," he repeated softly. "Which means I don't want to waste any time."

"I can't think straight when you kiss me like that," she complained.

His lips tilted crookedly. "I'll have to remember that. It might come in handy in the future."

Butterflies flew around inside her stomach. "Future?"

He grasped her ponytail and gently tugged her head back until her eyes met his. "I want you. For now. For always."

Her vision turned watery, all over again. "You promise?"

His expression went soft. His thumbs brushed over her wet cheeks. "I promise." He kissed her gently. Slowly. And so sweetly that if her heart hadn't already been his, it would have fallen into his hands right then and there. "I even brought proof."

"What's that?"

He pulled her hands from his hair and kissed her knuckles. Then he tugged her toward the front door and threw it open. Wholly bemused, she looked out into the yard.

The two men she'd seen before were still standing outside the delivery truck. Mason waved at them. "You can start," he called.

"Will do, Mr. Hyde." The first guy swept a knife over the pallet and lifted something off the top.

Her lips parted as she realized what it was.

A white picket fence panel.

Mason turned her toward him. "I love you, Courtney Clay. Will you take my picket fence and all that goes with it?"

"I will." She threw her arms around him and laughed through her tears. "For the rest of our lives, I will."

Epilogue

They were married in the candlelit living room of her parents' house on Christmas Eve.

Courtney wore a simple white gown with her hair pulled back in a ponytail and looked like his own personal angel. Mason wore a dark blue suit and managed not to pull off his silvery tie, even though he wanted to.

Plato was too dignified to wear a ring of flowers around his neck, though both Chloe and Shelby gave it their best efforts to keep it on him. He was also kept pretty occupied during the ceremony, corralling Woof so she wouldn't run up the gold-and-silver-decorated Christmas tree that filled part of the room.

The entire family was there, and Coleman Black, too, who'd stood up as Mason's best man.

It was crowded and cozy, and even though Mason had worried that Courtney was only going along with the small, quickly planned ceremony to keep him happy, all he had to do was look at the glowing face of his bride after they'd slid their rings on each other's fingers to know that their wedding had been everything she'd wanted it to be.

And she was everything he'd ever wanted.

"Come here." The vows were said and Sawyer and Rebecca were busy handing out flutes of sparkling champagne. Taking advantage of everyone's distraction, Mason tugged Courtney toward the French doors that opened onto the deck overlooking the back of the property.

Her palm slid against his, and she gave him a knowing look. "It's cold out there. How do you intend to keep me warm, Mr. Hyde?"

He nudged her through the door and wrapped his arm around her. "I have a few ways, Mrs. Hyde."

She shivered and snuggled close into his chest. Her hands slipped beneath his jacket and her sparkling eyes met his. "And I do love those ways," she admitted throatily. "Have I told you today how much I love you?"

Desire was ripping through him. But there would be time for that. Plenty of time. "Agreeing to wear this—" he grabbed her hand and kissed her finger where the narrow platinum wedding band rested "—tells me a lot."

Her smile softened. "Agreeing to wear this—" she returned, finding his hand with hers and rubbing the ring on his finger "—tells me everything." She leaned into him again. "I wonder how quickly we can escape our own wedding without looking rude," she whispered.

He laughed softly. This woman was either going to keep him young or make him die a very old, very satisfied man. He took off his jacket and slid it around her shoulders before pulling a ring-sized box out of the lapel pocket. "I wanted to give you this."

Her lips parted. "Mason, I don't have my gift for you. It's back at the house. I should wait until you can open yours, too."

He just shook his head. "This *is* a gift for me. Open it now."

She nudged her finger against the thin, white satin ribbon that surrounded the box. "Is this by any chance an engagement ring?"

The box *had* contained the diamond ring she'd insisted she didn't need, telling him the only ring she cared about was a wedding band. And while he believed her, he still wanted her to have the diamonds that went with it.

He wanted her to have everything.

Which was why the ring was not actually in the box but in his pocket to give to her later.

"Open it and see."

"You're spoiling me," she told him wryly. But she pressed open the box anyway and gave a surprised "oh." She laughed a little, pulling out one of the familiar condom wrappers that he'd tucked inside in place of the ring. "It's empty." She pulled out another. She lifted her eyebrows. "They're *all* empty."

"I know." He lowered his head to whisper in her ear. "The only gift you need to give me now is that baby."

Her lips parted. She pulled back her head to stare into his eyes. "Are you sure?"

"Never more."

Her eyes glowed. She tucked the wrappers back in the box, closed it, then slid it back into its place inside his jacket. "Poor 37892. He never even knew he didn't have a chance against you."

"Good grief." Squire's distinctive drawl came through the door, making them both jump. "What're you doing out in the cold? Gonna turn into Popsicles if you're not careful." He jerked his head. "Get in here and drink some champagne so *I* can have some cake." Then he grinned and turned back into the house.

Courtney and Mason looked at each other.

He smiled. She giggled.

And hand in hand, they went inside.

* * * * *

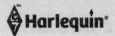
Harlequin®

REQUEST YOUR FREE BOOKS!
2 FREE NOVELS PLUS 2 FREE GIFTS!

SPECIAL EDITION
Life, Love & Family

Rafael de Luca had been in bad situations before. A crowded ballroom could never make him sweat.

These people would never know that he had no memory of any of them.

He surveyed the party with grim tolerance, searching for the source of his unease.

At first his gaze flickered past her, but he yanked his attention back to a woman across the room. Her stare bored holes through him. Unflinching and steady, even when his eyes locked with hers.

Petite, even in heels, she had a creamy olive complexion. A wealth of inky-black curls cascaded over her shoulders and her eyes were equally dark.

She looked at him as if she'd already judged him and found him lacking. He'd never seen her before in his life. Or had he?

He cursed the gaping hole in his memory. He'd been diagnosed with selective amnesia after his accident four months ago. Which seemed like complete and utter bull. No one got amnesia except hysterical women in bad soap operas.

With a smile, he disengaged himself from the group

around him and made his way to the mystery woman.

She wasn't coy. She stared straight at him as he approached, her chin thrust upward in defiance.

"Excuse me, but have we met?" he asked in his smoothest voice.

His gaze moved over the generous swell of her breasts pushed up by the empire waist of her black cocktail dress.

When he glanced back up at her face, he saw fury in her eyes.

"Have we *met?*" Her voice was barely a whisper, but he felt each word like the crack of a whip.

Before he could process her response, she nailed him with a right hook. He stumbled back, holding his nose.

One of his guards stepped between Rafe and the woman, accidentally sending her to one knee. Her hand flew to the folds of her dress.

It was then, as she cupped her belly, that the realization hit him. She was pregnant.

Her eyes flashing, she turned and ran down the marble hallway.

Rafael ran after her. He burst from the hotel lobby, and saw two shoes sparkling in the moonlight, twinkling at him.

He blew out his breath in frustration and then shoved the pair of sparkly, ultrafeminine heels at his head of security.

"Find the woman who wore these shoes."

Will Rafael find his mystery woman?
Find out in Maya Banks's passionate new novel
ENTICED BY HIS FORGOTTEN LOVER
Available September 2011 from Harlequin® Desire®!

Harlequin® Romance

Discover small-town warmth and community spirit
in a brand-new trilogy from

PATRICIA THAYER

The Quilt Shop in KERRY SPRINGS

*Where dreams
are stitched…patch
by patch!*

Coming August 9, 2011.

Little Cowgirl Needs a Mom

Warm-spirited quilt shop owner Jenny Collins promises to
help little Gracie finish the quilt her late mother started,
even if it means butting heads with Gracie's father,
grumpy but gorgeous rancher Evan Rafferty….

The Lonesome Rancher
(September 13, 2011)

Tall, Dark, Texas Ranger
(October 11, 2011)